CONFESSIONS

ALEX P. MOORE

Library of Congress Control Number: 2025915284

ISBN
978-1-967804-16-0 (Paperback)
978-1-967804-17-7 (eBook)
978-1-967804-15-3 (Hardcover)

TABLE OF CONTENTS

*A portrait of a devoted couple navigating
marriage, distance, and spiritual duty.*

*A traditional celebration full of joy and hope,
marking the beginning of a new chapter.*

*A joyful community gathering that reveals
character dynamics and social layers.*

*Ava and Adam welcome their son Daniel,
deepening their bond and responsibilities.*

*A spiritual milestone that reflects the
family's faith and communal ties.*

*Insights from Ava's father, a thoughtful
figure who brings quiet wisdom.*

PREFACE

This is not just a story about love—it is a confession of everything love must endure to remain pure.

Confessions opens in a forgotten European village, where time ticks in seasons and prayers, and where Ava and Adam—two souls wounded by tragedy—find something rare and holy in each other: a love so deep it stirs the soul and shakes the heavens. In this place of modesty and faith, their romance blossoms not with spectacle but with a sacred reverence. Bound by Church law and unrelenting devotion, they are drawn into the rites of courtship, chastity, marriage, and parenthood—each moment cloaked in both sanctity and sacrifice.

But love in this story is not idyllic. It is tested, bruised, and crucified.

When poverty and danger come knocking, Adam is forced to make an impossible choice: stay with the family he treasures or leave for America to secure their future. Their separation becomes not just a physical exile but a spiritual trial—a crucible where faith, fidelity, and desire battle against loneliness, temptation, and doubt.

Through whispered prayers, aching memories, and the raw, inner dialogue of two people clinging to a promise, *Confessions* invites you to witness a deeply human saga. At its heart are questions as old as time: How far would you go for love? How much would you sacrifice for faith? And can the human spirit remain unbroken when stretched across oceans and years?

This work is written in the tradition of spiritual realism—where God is present in every silence, and sin whispers even at the holiest of altars. It challenges the notion of romantic idealism and dares to confess what most are afraid to admit: that true love, like true faith, is not proven in easy moments, but in the suffering, longing, and lonely resolve to remain.

This is their story.

This is their confession.

AVA AND ADAM

A portrait of a devoted couple navigating marriage, distance, and spiritual duty.

In a forgotten corner of Eastern Europe, nestled between fields of wildflowers and crumbling cobblestone streets, stood a village untouched by time. Here, life was measured not in minutes or hours, but by the seasons of scent and blossom—pink cherry trees bursting with perfume in early spring, followed by the golden flood of linden blooms, whose fragrance clung to the air like a prayer. Winters were fierce and crystalline, and the villagers—weathered but full of spirit—glided on sleds and skates across frozen rivers, their laughter echoing like hymns.

It was a hard life. Work was scarce, wages meager. Yet the people endured, bound by the rhythms of the Church and the unspoken promises of family. In this place of tradition and tenacity, Ava arrived—lost, grieving, and alone.

Ava had come in the wake of unspeakable tragedy. A train derailment had stolen both her parents in a single violent moment.

As their only child, she bore the weight of loss with a silence that grew louder by the day. Her soul floated somewhere between numbness and despair. When kind neighbors intervened, they suggested she leave the city behind and seek solace with her widowed cousin, Therese, in a village distant enough to quiet the noise of memory.

Therese welcomed her with grace. Tall and slender, with hazel eyes and a quiet strength, Therese was raising her daughter, Dora, alone. In both mother and child, Ava found comfort—and slowly, the seeds of healing took root. With a degree in early childhood education and Therese's encouragement, Ava accepted a teaching position at the local preschool. The children became her balm. Their laughter, their wide-eyed wonder, breathed life back into her hollowed chest. Day by day, grief released its grip.

Ava herself was a vision—hair like molten copper, cascading in ringlets down her back; eyes the hue of a clear summer sky; a presence both ethereal and grounded. Songs could be written about her beauty. And perhaps they would be. But what made her radiant was not appearance alone—it was the quiet way she began to live again.

One misty morning, the sky hung low and soft rain kissed the earth. As she made her way to school, fog curling around her, she was lost in thought when a figure suddenly dropped from above. A man—tall, strong—slid down an electrical pole with the ease of a circus performer and landed squarely in her path.

Startled, she gasped. But only for a moment. His eyes—deep, warm, impossibly brown—met hers, and the world seemed to still. His face was sculpted, arresting; a mortal echo of a mythic god. For an instant, neither spoke. It was as if the air itself held its breath.

"Good morning," he finally said, his voice a soft baritone. "My name is Adam. Be careful walking here. The road winds in strange ways. And around here, speeding is more of a hobby than a hazard."

She smiled faintly, almost dazed. "I'm Ava. It's... very nice to meet you."

He extended his hand. She took it—and in that single touch, something ancient stirred. It was the spark of first creation, of soul meeting soul before memory began. For a moment, they stood motionless, electricity humming between them. Instinctively, they leaned toward each other, compelled by a force larger than reason—but quickly stepped back, breathless.

Adam began calling on her often. Their conversations, at first cautious, soon deepened. What began with glances and gentle laughter bloomed into a courtship rooted in faith and restraint. One kiss—tender, unforgettable—changed everything. It was enough to unravel them. They burned for each other, but kept themselves bound to their shared conviction: they would not break God's law.

Still, Adam could hardly resist the pull of her. Her hair—those flaming ringlets—seemed made for his hands. At times, he would catch himself stroking her cheek or brushing against her curves, only to stop himself, trembling at the edge of desire.

Marriage, then, was not just a promise. It was a necessity. A sanctuary. A sacred place where they could finally become one.

THE WEDDING

*A traditional celebration full of joy and hope,
marking the beginning of a new chapter.*

And so it came to this—Ava stood bathed in morning light, stepping carefully into the legacy of generations. Her wedding gown, lovingly preserved across time, had once belonged to her great-great-grandmother. The lace, yellowed to a shade just warmer than cream, whispered secrets of a century of love stories. Tiny hand-sewn roses and delicate ribbons danced across the fabric like faded memories. Pearls—real, lustrous—were stitched with reverence, their shimmer still unyielding after all these years.

She slipped her feet into high-button shoes worn by the women of her bloodline on the day they pledged their hearts. They pinched, slightly smaller than her usual size, but the leather—aged, soft as breath—embraced her like a mother's touch. She winced once, smiled, and whispered to herself, *"It's worth it. They all walked this path. Now it's my turn."*

Her hair—fiery, free—tumbled down her back in cascading red ringlets. A crown of tiny wildflowers nestled on her head, mirroring the delicate ribbons that trailed behind her like a whispered vow. Her face, radiant and flushed with anticipation, seemed to glow from within. A slow tremble stirred through her, not of fear, but of desire, joy, and the kind of love that rewrites a woman's soul.

Today, she would give herself to Adam.

They would begin their life together not alone but rooted in the warmth of family. His parents—kind, open-hearted, with laughter in their eyes—had embraced her like a daughter. There was no fear. No second thoughts. Only the electric pulse of something sacred.

As she stepped outside, the sun greeted her like an old friend. A path of fresh flowers lined the walkway from Therese's cottage to the car. Therese—her tireless cousin, her quiet savior—and little Dora, beautiful in her pale blue dress, were waiting by the door. Ava climbed into the gray sedan, her dress rustling softly like pages of a holy book.

At the church, everything shimmered. The wedding march began, and her heart pounded against her ribs like a drum of glory. The church—an eighteenth-century treasure—welcomed her with reverent silence and sunlight slanting through stained glass. She had always admired its carved wooden altar, burnished by time and touch. On the left stood Our Lady, garlanded with lilies. On the right, Saint Joseph held a lily of his own, guardian of purity and devotion.

Every pew was filled. Friends from the village. Parents of the children she taught. Strangers whose lives she had unknowingly touched. They had come to witness something rare.

She longed to kneel and pray, but the weight of the moment overtook her. The only words that came were whispered from the bottom of her soul:

"Jesus, help."

Dora led the procession, a basket of petals in hand, scattering soft reds and whites like blessings before a queen. Therese followed—strong, proud, holding Ava's courage in her gaze. And then it was Ava's turn.

Tears welled in her eyes, unbidden. She thought of her parents—how they should have been here. How they would have wept with joy. The ache stabbed through her chest, sharp and fleeting—until she saw him.

Adam.

He stood tall beneath the arch of the altar, a vision of strength and promise. Golden-haired, broad-shouldered, dressed in a deep blue suit that molded to his body like it had been stitched by angels. But it was his eyes—warm, steady, searching only for her—that unmade her completely.

He extended his hand. She reached out—and the moment they touched, the world fell away.

She was his. Entirely. Eternally.

They knelt, trembling, before the altar.

During the homily, Father Thomas's voice rang out through the incense-laced air like a prophecy.

"Love," he said, "is the greatest gift one soul can offer another. Not money. Not power. Not even time. Love is the very breath of God. It strengthens where the body fails. It forgives where pride would punish.

To fall in love is to expose your truest self, without fear. From this day on, Ava and Adam, you are no longer two, but one. Share everything—your joys, your burdens, your dreams. Be faithful. Be fruitful. Let your love echo across generations.

And may your children carry it forward as a legacy born of truth and fire."

Ava bowed her head, clutching Adam's hand. She had come through fire and shadow to arrive at this altar. Now, dressed in the memory of her foremothers and the faith of her heart, she stepped fully into her destiny.

THE PARTY

*A joyful community gathering that reveals
character dynamics and social layers.*

After the sacred hush of the ceremony, the village came alive with laughter and clinking glasses. Outside the old stone church, just across the courtyard, stood a modest hall—used for wedding receptions, parish meetings, and the occasional funeral meal. Today, it pulsed with joy.

Before joining the celebration, Adam discreetly handed Father Thomas an envelope containing a heartfelt offering—his way of honoring the man who had blessed the most important moment of his life. Tucked alongside it was an invitation: "Please, join us, Father. Tonight, we celebrate not only our marriage, but God's grace."

Father Thomas nodded solemnly. "It would be my joy."

The hall had been transformed by love and care. Though humble in structure—whitewashed walls, wooden beams, and aged flooring—it glowed. Candles flickered in glass holders, their soft light dancing across holy icons that adorned every wall. Some were framed paintings of saints, others delicate carvings in wood or fired ceramic—each one a silent witness to countless rites of passage.

Round tables filled the room, each draped in ivory linen embroidered with traditional village patterns—spirals, crosses, and blooming flowers in crimson thread. At the center of each table stood a small glass vase filled with red carnations and baby's breath, a simple but elegant nod to old-world beauty. The dishes matched the linens—ceramic, hand-painted, no two exactly the same.

Father Thomas was seated at a table near the front, surrounded by a mix of younger villagers and elders eager for his company. In their culture, it was a rare and revered thing— to dine at the same table as the priest. It wasn't just respect; it was intimacy. This was not a time for distant reverence. It was a time for communion, for questions, for truths.

Wine flowed, and so did curiosity.

A young woman in a lace shawl leaned forward, eyes gleaming. "Father, may I ask… when does kissing become a sin?"

A ripple of laughter moved through the table, but Father Thomas did not smile. He answered with calm sincerity.

"There are many kinds of kisses," he said. "The kiss of a child to her mother, the kiss between siblings, even the kiss of peace during Mass—these are pure, born of love. But if a kiss is given only for arousal, without true love or commitment, then it can become a kind of theft. A pleasure taken, not shared. Do not forget," he added quietly, "it was with a kiss that Judas betrayed our Lord."

The table fell quiet. A young man in a crisp blue jacket cleared his throat. "Then, Father… how can we explore sexuality without falling into sin?"

Father Thomas studied him. "You must wait. Wait until you are married. Sexual union is sacred—it is not a game, not something to be practiced, but something to be given entirely. To begin this act and not complete it within marriage... is to break the holy design."

"But Father," another voice chimed in, this time from a shy girl with auburn braids, "can a married couple use contraception if they don't want children right away?"

Father Thomas frowned. "No. Never. That is not God's plan. You may only use natural methods. Contraception closes the door to life, and life is God's greatest gift. To deny it is to deny Him."

There was a murmur of unease, a ripple of real-world frustration that clashed with spiritual idealism. Then an older man, his suit well-fitted and his voice wearied by experience, spoke up.

"Father, I work. I travel. I give to the church as best I can. My wife and I love each other deeply, but at forty, with four children already, we must abstain during her fertile times. It's hard, Father. We're tired. We love each other. We want to be together. How can we do this without sinning?"

Father Thomas nodded slowly. "Marriage is not just a union of bodies, but a covenant of sacrifice. I understand your pain. But understand this—self-restraint is not punishment. It's preparation. The joy that comes after waiting is often greater than any fleeting pleasure. God sees your struggle. And in that struggle, you are sanctified."

Then, from the far end of the table, a frail woman with weathered skin and watery eyes asked softly, "Father... what happens if we fail? If we cannot bear the wait?"

There was a long silence. Then Father Thomas said simply, "Then we go to confession. And we try again."

Ava watched this exchange from her seat near the head table, Adam's warm hand resting over hers. She felt the strange pull of ancient truth and modern yearning swirling around them. This was not just a party. It was a passage. A crossing from innocence to adulthood, from theory to flesh, from ritual to reality.

As the meal continued, violins began to play in the corner of the room. The voices rose again—lighter now, warmed by food, wine, and the shared knowledge that faith, like marriage, was not about perfection.

It was about persistence.

And tonight, beneath the eyes of saints and under the ceiling of heaven, a new chapter had begun.

FIRST CHILD

Ava and Adam welcome their son Daniel, deepening their bond and responsibilities.

While the party still stirred with laughter and conversation, Ava and Adam sat close together at their table, their bodies still and formal, but their eyes… their eyes burned with a silent, restrained hunger.

"Soon, my love," Adam whispered, his breath warm against her ear, "we'll discover what we've only dreamed of—what we barely held back for so long."

Ava blushed, her heart fluttering. She had waited. They both had. And now, everything was sacred, everything blessed.

When the last dish was cleared and the final guests embraced them with parting blessings, Ava and Adam returned to the house they now shared with his parents. The small upper room had been lovingly prepared—fresh linens, a simple bouquet on the windowsill, and lace curtains billowing gently in the evening breeze. As they closed the door behind them, Momma and Papa exchanged a knowing glance. Their smiles held stories of their own wedding night, long ago. They loved Ava like a daughter, and tonight, they thanked God for the joy their son had found.

Behind that closed door, vows gave way to fire. The first time was hesitant—a little pain, a gasp, then Adam's trembling kiss easing her fear, reassuring them both. He, too, was discovering, and together they fumbled into something raw, beautiful, and holy. With every touch they shed layers of restraint and modesty until only their truest selves remained.

His hands set her skin alight. She arched beneath him, undone by the power she held in her embrace. And when he entered her—sudden, rough, desperate—she cried out, not in pain, but in glory. That night, they made love over and over, until exhaustion became sleep and sleep gave way to sunrise.

Their days unfolded like pages in a psalm. Evenings ended with shared rosaries beside Momma and Papa, their whispered prayers mingling with candlelight and gratitude. They were not wealthy. Their home was modest, their salaries humble. But they were rich in love, and their hearts beat in harmony with God's design.

Two months later, as Adam returned from work—his boots dusty, his shirt damp with labor—Ava ran to greet him. She flung her arms around his neck and held him tightly, almost trembling.

"Adam," she said breathlessly, eyes shining, "we're going to have a baby."

For a moment, he said nothing. His eyes widened, his lips parted, and then—laughter, soft and stunned, like a child's first breath.

"Ava… my darling… a baby?" he whispered, pressing his forehead to hers. "Have you told Momma and Papa?"

"I wanted us to tell them together. Tonight. During the rosary… let's offer it in thanksgiving for the life we've created."

That evening, beneath the flickering glow of their family altar, their secret bloomed into joy. Momma wept openly. Papa bowed his head, murmuring a quiet prayer of thanks. A new life—God's promise—was already stirring beneath Ava's heart.

Pregnancy suited her. She remained healthy and serene, continuing to teach at the preschool until the final week. Adam watched her in awe—stroking her growing belly, whispering prayers into her skin.

"Does it hurt when he moves?" he asked, eyes wide with wonder.

"No," she smiled, "it's like a gentle flutter. It comforts me."

"So it *is* a boy, then!" he declared with a grin.

"Perhaps," she teased. "But would it matter?"

"Not at all. Boy or girl… they are ours. A miracle. We are co-creators with God."

When labor began, the midwife was summoned. Ava bore the pain with quiet strength, and in just under three hours, their child entered the world—a healthy, howling eight-pound boy. They named him **Daniel**.

Adam fell to his knees at her bedside, tears streaming down his face as he held Ava's hand in one and their child in the other.

"Thank You, Lord," he whispered. "Thank You for keeping them safe."

Momma and Papa knelt beside him, voices trembling as they prayed in thanksgiving.

Later that evening, Adam slipped away to the church, still overcome. He needed to speak to Father Thomas about the baptism, to begin their son's journey of faith. But the parish housekeeper met him at the door.

"Father Thomas has gone to meet with the Bishop," she said gently. "He won't return until morning."

Adam nodded. "It's important, but not urgent. I'll return after work tomorrow."

"Congratulations," she said, smiling warmly. "A child is God's greatest blessing." She handed him a wrapped package. "Here. A lemon chiffon cake. It's for your family, to celebrate."

Grateful, Adam cradled the gift and stepped back into the golden light of dusk. The sky was clear. Birds were singing. He walked quickly, almost running, eager to be home before visitors arrived—before Daniel woke—before any moment of this miraculous day could slip away.

When he stepped through the front door, he called softly, "Ava?"

"Shhh," she answered, peeking out from the bedroom. "He's just fallen asleep. Did you speak with Father?"

"No," Adam said, setting the cake down gently, "he's away until tomorrow. But I'll return. We have time. I think two weeks is perfect for the baptism."

"Any news on the job?" she asked hopefully.

"Not yet. But maybe tomorrow." He lifted the cake. "Meanwhile, the housekeeper sent us this."

Ava chuckled, "We'll feast like royalty tonight." Then her voice softened, "I'm still sore... but I feel okay. Just tired."

Adam leaned in, giving her a mischievous smile. "In a week or two, I'll take care of those sore places." He pulled her into his arms, and together they stood at the kitchen window, watching lace curtains sway in the soft breeze, the horizon stretched out like a promise.

In her heart, Ava thanked God again. For Adam. For Daniel. For every breath.

Yet worry tugged quietly at her thoughts. *His job is dangerous. The pay is low. What if something happens to him?* He was more than her husband—he was her heart, her friend, her whole world.

That night, after feeding Daniel and tucking him into his cradle, she lit a candle at their bedroom altar and whispered a prayer beneath her breath:

"Mother Mary, protect him. Bring him a better job, a safer one. I can endure anything, but not the loss of him."

Several days later, Adam returned to the church and arranged Daniel's baptism for the following Sunday. It gave Ava and Momma time to prepare the food and clean the house for the guests. Choosing the godparents was easy. Their neighbor, Joseph—a devout, honest man—was perfect for Godfather. Therese, Ava's cousin and closest confidante, would be Godmother. She had helped with laundry, stayed up late rocking Daniel, and loved the child already as if he were her own.

Both were devout Catholics. Both would protect Daniel's soul.

The family was ready. The child had arrived. And in a world of struggle, faith, and love—hope was alive.

DANIEL'S BAPTISM

The sun rose on the day of Daniel's baptism like a golden benediction, warm and full of promise. The village, quiet in the early hours, seemed to hold its breath. The air was rich with the scent of baking bread and morning dew, as if heaven itself had leaned down to kiss the earth.

Ava stood by the window, rocking Daniel gently in her arms. He was swaddled in white—the same christening gown Adam had worn as an infant, lovingly preserved by Momma. Tiny pearl buttons fastened down the front, and delicate lace trimmed the sleeves. His eyes were wide, as if he sensed the weight of the day. Ava pressed her lips to his forehead and whispered a silent prayer.

In the kitchen, Adam was helping his mother finish the final touches for the celebration meal. Outside, Papa was setting up chairs beneath the tree where the guests would gather after the ceremony. The day felt holy.

The godparents arrived just after mid-morning.

Joseph, their neighbor of many years, wore a charcoal gray suit and a quiet air of pride. He was shorter than Adam but broad-shouldered, with a raw-boned frame hardened by years of labor. His eyes were kind, his smile always ready. Wherever he went, he was greeted warmly—by merchants, priests, politicians alike. He had a reputation not only as a hard worker but as someone who knew how to get things done.

What Adam didn't know—what no one ever said aloud— was exactly what Joseph did for a living. He mentioned "construction," but there were whispers of connections, favors, and quiet influence. Still, Joseph had never shown anything but loyalty and generosity, and Adam trusted him. He was a good man. A reliable friend.

Joan, Joseph's wife, arrived shortly after him, her expression carved in tight lines. She rarely smiled. Plump and practical, she bustled more than she spoke. Though her demeanor was cold, her intentions were never cruel. She brought with her a tray of rich pastries, still warm, and a tightly folded napkin embroidered with Ava's name.

She was a woman of duty, not affection.

Their marriage, though long-standing, was brittle. From the beginning, Joan had recoiled from intimacy. Even in the early days, Joseph's affection had been met with discomfort, resistance. After two children and years of quiet frustration, the bedroom grew silent. Arguments followed. Long silences. Joseph, though faithful, ached for connection. In time, he buried that ache in work—long hours, official dealings, whispered alliances. He provided well. He kept his vows. But the longing never left him.

Still, today was not about sorrow. Today was about Daniel.

The church was full of loved ones and parishioners. The carved altars glowed with candles. Flowers lined the aisle—lilies and white roses—and the scent of incense curled in lazy tendrils toward the vaulted ceiling.

A hush fell over the congregation as Father Thomas approached the baptismal font. He was resplendent in gold and white vestments, his expression solemn but gentle.

Ava and Adam stepped forward, Daniel nestled in Adam's arms. Joseph and Therese followed as godparents, reverent and still. Father Thomas raised his hand and began the rite.

"We gather today in great joy, as we welcome this child—Daniel—into the body of Christ. Two weeks ago, he entered the world. Today, he is reborn into grace."

As the water touched Daniel's forehead, he did not cry. Instead, he blinked, serene and silent, as if he understood what had been bestowed upon him.

"Daniel, I baptize you in the name of the Father, and of the Son, and of the Holy Spirit…"

The congregation murmured a collective Amen.

Then Father Thomas lifted his hands and spoke:

"This child is now a member of the Church. It will be your duty—Ava, Adam, Joseph, and Therese—to raise him in the light of God. Teach him to pray. Teach him to serve. One day, he will build up the Kingdom of God with his own hands—through faith, through labor, and through love."

Ava wept quietly. Adam bowed his head, overcome. Therese held her breath, and Joseph… Joseph stood stiffly, something unreadable in his eyes. Watching Adam and Ava, holding their newborn with joy, stirred something in him that he could not name. A longing. A regret.

After the ceremony, Ava and Adam approached Father Thomas and handed him a small envelope, their way of saying thank you. He accepted it graciously and was soon escorted to the head table at the feast.

The celebration back at the house was vibrant. Neighbors filled the yard. Wine was poured. Children ran barefoot through the grass. Laughter echoed. Joan served her pastries. Joseph poured drinks. And through it all, Adam kept one hand on Ava's back and the other gently cradling Daniel's tiny head.

They had very little. Their home was modest, their future uncertain. But in this moment, surrounded by prayer and the fragrance of roast lamb and cinnamon cakes, they had everything that mattered.

And though Ava smiled and greeted guests, part of her heart was already whispering to God again:

"Protect us. Let him live to see Daniel grow. Let our son know his father. Let this peace last."

Little did they know, beyond the borders of this joyful day, storms were already forming—quietly, invisibly—waiting to test the very love they had just blessed.

PATIENT PHILOSOPHER

Insights from Ava's father, a thoughtful figure who brings quiet wisdom.

First Day

The storm outside raged with a bitter vengeance—snow driven sideways by the wind, rattling windowpanes and sealing the town in ice. But not even weather like this could keep **Father Felix** from his hospital rounds. He walked the short two-block path from the rectory through snowdrifts nearly to his knees, his cassock flapping like a black flag of defiance against the cold.

He had not missed a day in twelve years.

On the north wing of the hospital, in a dimly lit four-bed ward, a **new patient** had been admitted. As was his custom, Father Felix made his way to each bedside with a kind word and a blessing, saving the new face for last.

As he neared the final bed, the other patients subtly signaled to him—waves, raised brows, a few half-winks. He smiled warmly, lifting his hand in blessing, assuming they were merely greeting him with affection. But he would soon understand there was something more—something unsaid behind their gestures.

The man in the final bed was tall, elderly, with sunken cheeks and thinning white hair. His eyes, once blue, were now pale and clouded like ice over water.

Father Felix gently pulled the curtain around the bed, shielding them from the room's distractions and the cold wind that seeped through the window.

"Peace be with you," Father Felix said quietly. "I'm Father Felix. How are you feeling, my brother?"

The man turned slowly toward him. His breath came in short, ragged bursts.

"You're wasting your time," he rasped. "I don't believe in priests."

Father Felix didn't flinch. "You don't need to believe in priests," he said gently. "Your faith belongs to God."

The man closed his eyes. "I was never... a communist... nor a party man... I never condemned the Church... or priests..." Each word came between gasps. "I was baptized... First Communion... even Confirmed... But God?" His voice cracked. "No. I do not believe."

Father Felix moved closer, his tone steady. "Then perhaps I am here not as a priest... but as a companion. If you're willing to speak, I'm willing to listen."

The man opened his eyes again. They were glassy but aware.

"I was eight... the Pastor had a garden... it smelled like paradise. Apples. I couldn't help myself—I climbed the fence... stole a few... sweetest I'd ever tasted."

He paused, chest heaving.

"But the Pastor caught me. He told my parents. They beat me with a belt, hard. My back bled. I was ashamed...

humiliated… and that night, sitting in the dark corner of my room, I decided something…"

He looked directly at Father Felix.

"I decided… it is impossible."

"What is impossible?" the priest asked gently.

"That a God could allow such cruelty. Over apples. What kind of God stands by while a child is beaten for hunger? For curiosity? No. No God would allow that."

The silence between them stretched.

"And so, I began to search—not for proof of God's existence—but for proof of his **nonexistence**."

Father Felix nodded solemnly. "Then you are a true philosopher, my brother. And yes—I have time to listen. As much as you need."

"Tomorrow… maybe…" the man whispered. "I'm tired now."

"Rest well," said Father Felix, placing his hand gently on the man's shoulder. "And may God bless you—whether you believe in Him or not."

SECOND DAY

Father Felix returned the next afternoon. The storm had passed, leaving behind a white stillness. The hospital felt strangely holy in its silence.

The man was sitting up slightly, his breathing less labored.

"Hello, Father…"

"I'm glad to see you're stronger. Shall we continue our conversation?"

"Yes," the man said with a faint smile. "I was married once. We had three children. My wife raised them Catholic. I never interfered. I never argued against the Church. But I didn't push them either."

He paused, choosing his next words carefully.

"While my wife raised them in faith… I was searching. For meaning. For truth. I read the great philosophers. I studied religions—not to believe—but to disprove. I found them all… man-made."

He coughed, struggling to speak.

"Philosophy, I concluded, is written by people… **for** people. Religion? Invented by priests… to control the ignorant."

Father Felix remained still, his face unreadable.

"But the universe," the man continued, his eyes now distant, "the universe is different. It is vast. Unimaginable. Trillions of stars. Billions of galaxies. Life, I believe, is an accident. We are grains of sand on an infinite shore. No divine hand required. No God. Just… possibility."

And then, once again, he said the words:

"It is impossible."

"What is impossible this time?" Father Felix asked quietly.

"That God created it. That He knows us. That He cares about any of us."

The priest clasped his hands. "Still you search. Still you question. But remember, my brother… faith is not about proof. If it were, it would be knowledge, not belief."

The man closed his eyes. "Tomorrow, then…"

"Tomorrow," Father Felix agreed.

THIRD DAY

Father Felix arrived at the hospital with the early morning chill still clinging to his coat. A sense of anticipation tugged at his spirit. His thoughts had been restless through the night— haunted not by doubt, but by concern. There was something unfinished… something fragile hovering near the edge.

He stepped into the familiar ward, his eyes moving instinctively toward the corner bed.

It was empty.

The sheets were stripped. The pillow stacked neatly.

A hollow thud echoed in his chest.

He turned quickly to the nurse at the desk. "Where is my patient—the elderly man in bed four?"

The nurse looked up, slightly startled by his tone. "Oh. He was moved during the night—to a private room at the end of the hall. Room 208. He took a turn for the worse. Oxygen dropped. They didn't think he'd make it to morning."

Without a word, Father Felix turned and rushed down the corridor, the hem of his cassock snapping behind him. Fluorescent lights flickered above, and the scent of antiseptic filled his lungs.

Room 208.

He flung open the door.

There, under a dim bedside lamp, lay the patient—his philosopher. His body was barely more than a shadow beneath the white sheets. His face had turned an ashen hue, skin drawn tight over cheekbones, lips tinged with blue. Only the faint rise and fall of his chest marked the fragile thread of life still clinging to him.

Father Felix's breath caught. He was dying.

There was no time to wait for equipment or protocol. The priest dropped to his knees beside the bed, pulled the small vial of oil from his coat pocket, and gently anointed the man's forehead, then each of his palms—his hands trembling, his voice steady.

"Through this holy anointing, may the Lord in His love and mercy help you with the grace of the Holy Spirit…"

His voice thickened as he continued:

"May the Lord who frees you from sin… save you… and raise you up."

He signed the cross gently over the man's brow.

For a brief moment, the man's eyes fluttered. A faint groan escaped his lips—whether pain or recognition, Felix couldn't tell. But something passed between them.

A moment of mystery.

Then Felix sprang to his feet and sprinted down the hallway to the nurses' station.

"You need to check on the man in Room 208—immediately! He's slipping away!"

The nurse's eyes widened. "No one updated us… We weren't even monitoring him yet. He wasn't on the critical list."

She grabbed a vitals kit and rushed down the hall, followed by two aides.

As Felix stood watching them disappear into the room, his hand rested on the wooden counter.

He closed his eyes briefly.

He had arrived just in time.

Or perhaps, God had.

FOURTH DAY

Father Felix arrived at the hospital earlier than usual, his breath fogging in the morning air as he hurried through the entrance, heart restless with anticipation. He had scarcely slept the night before, haunted by the pale face of his philosopher patient— hovering somewhere between belief and eternity.

As he stepped into the ward, the fluorescent lights hummed softly above, casting a sterile glow on the freshly mopped floors. A few nurses at the main station looked up and smiled.

"Good morning, Father," one of them said. "You came just in time yesterday."

He paused, uncertain. "What do you mean?"

The head nurse, a stout woman with tired eyes and a clipped tone, looked up from her clipboard. "That man in room 208—the one you visited? We didn't realize how close he was to coding. He wasn't even hooked up to a monitor. No alert. Nothing."

Another nurse added, "You found him just in time. If you hadn't… well… it might've been a very different morning."

Father Felix's chest tightened with a quiet, holy weight. He nodded solemnly.

"It wasn't me," he said softly. "It was Providence."

The nurse tilted her head. "Maybe so. But whatever it was, you bought him a little more time."

Felix made his way down the long corridor, passing the very ward where he had first met the man. The bed was already occupied by someone else—an old woman asleep with her mouth slightly open, snoring gently.

Room 208. The door was slightly ajar.

He pushed it open.

Inside, the room was still. The blinds were partially drawn, letting in ribbons of pale winter light. Machines hummed quietly in the background. The man was there—his body now connected to wires, his breathing more even. His chest rose and fell slowly, his hands lying still at his sides.

Father Felix approached the bed and stood in silence for a long moment. The man's face was peaceful, but wan—like a candle burning low. There was a flicker of consciousness beneath his closed eyelids, but he didn't stir.

Felix whispered a quiet prayer.

"You're not alone," he said gently. "Not now. Not ever."

In his heart, he knew: yesterday had not been a coincidence. That sacred moment, the whisper of near-death, the conditional anointing—it had been a divine intersection, a lifeline cast at the very edge of eternity.

He had not come simply to speak with a skeptic. He had come to catch a soul.

FIFTH DAY

The man's eyes were open again—weak, but aware.

"Welcome back, my friend," said Father Felix. "Yesterday I anointed you. Was that all right?"

The man coughed. His voice was thin as thread.

"It is… impossible…"

"What now is impossible, my brother?"

"That we die… like animals. That's it? Nothing after?"

His chest rose slowly.

"There has to be something more… There **must** be something after this…"

"Do you believe, now, in eternal life?"

A pause. A breath.

"Yes," the man whispered. "I do."

"And in God?"

Another breath. "Yes, I believe."

Father Felix smiled.

"Are you sorry for your sins?"

Tears gathered in the corners of the man's eyes.

"I am… deeply sorry."

"Then you have confessed."

"But I need to confess properly…"

"You just did," Father Felix said gently. "And I absolve you, in the name of the Father, and of the Son, and of the Holy Spirit."

"Amen," the man whispered.

Father Felix then gave him **Holy Communion**—his first in over fifty years, and his last.

SIXTH DAY

The next morning, Father Felix pushed open the doors of the hospital with a strange stillness in his spirit. The snow had melted into slush overnight, and gray light filtered through the clouds like breath held in suspense. He didn't know why—but he already felt it. Something in the air was different.

He made his way to the second floor, his steps slower than usual, his cassock brushing against the floor in rhythmic sways. The hospital corridor was unusually quiet. Even the nurses at the station, usually bustling with reports and clipped instructions, seemed subdued—solemn.

He looked toward Room 208. The door stood open.

The bed was empty.

No medical monitors. No pale blue sheets. Just stillness.

Before he could ask, the head nurse met his eyes. She said nothing at first. She didn't need to. Her expression—soft, reverent—told the truth before her lips did.

"He passed… just after midnight," she said quietly. "Peacefully. A couple hours after you left."

Felix felt the words sink deep into his chest like a stone into calm water. He closed his eyes, breathed in slowly, and whispered, "Thank You, Lord."

The nurse touched his forearm gently. "He was calm. His breathing slowed, then just… stopped. No fear. No pain. He passed like someone falling asleep."

Father Felix nodded, lips pressed together in bittersweet understanding. He offered a silent blessing with his hand, then turned and walked slowly down the hallway, his footsteps echoing like a fading heartbeat.

He entered the hospital chapel, a tiny room tucked behind frosted glass doors. It was empty.

He made his way to the front, knelt before the crucifix, and lowered his head. The silence enveloped him like a sacred veil.

And then the tears came.

Not tears of sorrow—but of awe. Of thankfulness. Of sacred wonder.

He wept for the mystery of it all—the long war between doubt and belief, between pride and surrender, and for the miraculous grace that finds us even in our final breath.

A soul that had once declared, *"It is impossible,"* had died whispering, *"I believe."*

Father Felix raised his eyes to the wooden cross above him, and a quiet smile played at the corners of his lips.

One more soul had returned home.

SECOND CHILD

*The birth of their daughter Margaret
brings balance and joy.*

Life settled into a fragile rhythm for Adam and Ava. Daniel, now toddling around on unsteady legs, was the light of the household—always giggling, always reaching for his Papa the moment he walked through the door. Adam would scoop him up and toss him in the air, just to hear that unrestrained baby laugh that made everything else—poverty, fatigue, uncertainty—fade for a while.

But today was different.

Adam stepped into the house just before dusk, smelling faintly of burnt insulation and smoke. His eyebrows were singed, his hair uneven, his hands wrapped in makeshift bandages. Ava looked up from folding laundry and gasped.

"Adam!" she rushed to him, "What happened to you?"

He tried to wave her off. "Nothing. Just a small mishap at work. I'm fine."

But Ava's voice rose, trembling. "Don't lie to me. Your hair—it's burnt! And your hands—look at them! You've been hurt! What kind of job does this to a man?"

He tried to smile, but it faltered beneath the weight of her gaze. "It was just… a small shock. I wasn't careful. But it's better pay."

"Better pay?" Her eyes widened. "Adam, you could've been killed!"

He wanted to confess it all—that he had been thrown back by an arc of live electricity, that he saw white light before darkness nearly swallowed him—but Ava was already pale, her free hand resting gently on her abdomen, swollen now with the new life growing within her.

"I'm fine," he lied gently. "It looks worse than it is. Really."

She stared at him for a long moment, her eyes welling. "We weren't even trying for another baby… and you're out risking your life."

He kissed her forehead. "It'll be okay, Ava. We'll manage."

But in the silence of their shared room that night, Adam sat by the window long after Ava had fallen asleep, rocking Daniel in his arms. Outside, wild autumn winds rattled the shutters, whispering to him through the cracks, *You're not enough. You'll never be enough.*

His thoughts churned like a storm. Another mouth to feed. A dangerous job. A wife who was too tired to work much longer. Where would the money come from? Could he get a second job? There were none to be found. He felt the cold fingers of desperation wrapping around his chest again.

But on Wednesday evening, the entire family knelt inside the sanctuary of the church for Holy Hour, clinging to the stillness of prayer. The flicker of candles cast golden light on the statues of Mary and Joseph, and the sweet scent of incense lingered in the air. Adam found comfort in Therese's familiar face, in Joseph's calm presence, and in little Dora—no longer a child, now blossoming into a helpful young woman. He would ask Therese if Dora could help Ava when the time came.

Father Thomas led the rosary, but left quickly afterward. Someone mentioned he had urgent matters with the Bishop—parish growth, perhaps. There was talk of adding a new wing to the church school. Ava's strength would not allow her to return to teaching anytime soon, but perhaps one day, she might.

That evening, as they returned home through the wind-swept streets, Adam's mother watched him closely. She had noticed his gloved hands in church. She saw how short his hair had been clipped, how he recoiled slightly when she moved toward him.

"What's wrong with your face, Adam?" she asked gently.

"Nothing, Mama. Just tired."

But she narrowed her eyes and reached toward his cheek. He flinched. She said nothing—but she knew. She would pray harder that night.

His father, quiet and observant as always, said nothing. But he had seen the pain in his son's movements, the burns hidden under powder and ointment. He said nothing… yet his silence spoke volumes.

Then, a sharp cry pierced the room.

Ava hunched over, clutching her belly. Her face twisted in pain.

"It's too soon," she gasped. "It's not time yet."

The household erupted into motion. The midwife was called immediately. The minutes became hours. It was a long, harrowing labor—unlike her first. Ava bled heavily. Her cries echoed down the hallway as the storm outside grew more violent.

But just before dawn, a small, wet cry broke through the tension.

A girl.

Six pounds, two ounces. Red curls like Ava's, tightly coiled and glistening.

They named her **Margaret**.

Ava, pale and exhausted, drifted into a shallow sleep. The doctor came the next day and ordered her to bedrest. "No work. No lifting. You need to heal. This delivery… it was close," he warned. "And no more children anytime soon. Your body needs time."

Momma wept softly in the kitchen, rocking Daniel, while Papa sat at the table, holding his rosary beads, silently mouthing prayers of thanksgiving.

Adam stood by the crib, watching tiny Margaret breathe. Her chest rose and fell, perfect and serene. He reached down and touched her tiny fingers. She gripped one, instinctively.

He turned to Ava, asleep in bed, her skin still pale, her lips chapped from pain and fatigue. She looked like porcelain.

He felt the guilt again.

They had tried the Church's method—the calendar, the abstinence, the temperature readings, the nursing protection myth. On their bedroom door, Ava had carefully marked the calendar: **hearts** for safe days, **X's** for fertile ones. They followed the rules. And still, this child had come.

He felt both awe… and fear.

How would he protect them?

If dangerous jobs were the only ones that paid enough, he would take them. He would burn his hands again if he had to. He would walk into the storm and let it take him—so long as Ava and the children remained safe behind the door.

In his heart, he whispered a single plea:

"God… just give me the strength."

MARGARET'S BAPTISM

Six weeks after Margaret's difficult birth, Ava was finally strong enough to attend Mass and prepare for the ceremony. Though her body had mostly healed, her spirit still moved slowly, like a tree learning how to bloom again after a harsh winter.

The house was buzzing with quiet anticipation that morning. Adam had helped bathe little Margaret, who squirmed and giggled in the warm water, her red curls clinging to her cherubic cheeks. Wrapped in a hand-stitched white gown passed down from Ava's family, Margaret looked like a tiny angel. Her clear blue eyes blinked solemnly, already wise in some mysterious way.

Ava wore a simple blue dress and held Daniel's hand as they walked to the church. Her body was still tender, but her heart was full. Adam, ever protective, kept one arm around her and the other gently cradling the bundle in his arms.

The church was fragrant with lilies and wax, sunlight cutting through the stained glass windows in colors that danced across the marble floor. The ancient wooden pews creaked as family and neighbors filed in. Therese sat beside Dora, who beamed proudly—she was Margaret's godmother. Joseph, tall and serious as ever, stood beside the baptismal font, his hand resting gently on Daniel's shoulder.

Father Thomas stepped forward, his white vestments embroidered with gold thread. His voice, though aged, echoed with clarity.

"Money," he began, "does not bring happiness. True happiness comes from love... from the sacrifice and joy of family life. The child you bring forward today, Margaret, is not only your daughter, but a child of God. In baptism, she will be sealed with His promise, and charged to walk in faith. And you, Adam and Ava, are her first teachers in holiness. Be worthy of that honor."

The water, cool and sacred, flowed over Margaret's head. She made a small sound—not quite a cry, more a celestial murmur—and opened her eyes wide, as if she recognized something eternal in the act.

"Margaret Anne," Father Thomas said gently, "I baptize you in the name of the Father, and of the Son, and of the Holy Spirit."

"Amen," the congregation whispered.

Afterward, Adam pressed an envelope into the priest's hand, and Ava handed him a handwritten invitation to dinner. Father Thomas, glancing inside the envelope, saw more cash than usual. He murmured, "Good, good," with a quick flicker of satisfaction that darted across his face like a shadow. He caught himself, smiled broadly, and added in a more benevolent tone:

"Of course. Thank you. I will come. God bless you both. God bless this child."

As they walked back home, Ava leaned against Adam. "I'm so glad it's done," she whispered. "She's safe now. Sealed with God's grace."

But the undercurrent of worry never left her completely.

Money was tight. Ava returned to working part-time at the preschool, taking both children with her. Dora came often to help, carrying Margaret or playing with Daniel, who was more like Adam every day—gentle, observant, and brimming with quiet joy. Ava would sometimes pause in the middle of wiping noses or teaching songs just to watch her children play. They were her entire world.

But joy often sat side by side with dread.

Adam's job remained dangerous—more dangerous now than ever. Every day, he climbed poles, repaired high-voltage lines, braving winds and snow, or rain that could turn a misstep into death. He rarely spoke of the risks, but Ava saw it in the burns on his fingers, in the aching silence when he returned home late, in the way he sometimes stared out the window too long without blinking.

She feared for him. Every time he kissed her goodbye, she fought back tears, praying it wasn't the last.

Their nights were complicated.

They practiced abstinence—strictly. They could not afford another child. It had been too much for her body, too much for their strained finances. And though their love remained, the tension between their bodies simmered under the surface.

There were nights when they lay side by side, hearts pounding, hands searching, breath catching—but always stopping before the point of no return. They found fleeting release in whispered kisses and desperate touches. Oral pleasure helped ease the ache, but it did not erase the longing to be whole again.

The Church taught sacrifice, and they tried—God knew, they tried.

But abstinence grew like a wedge between them. Some nights they quarreled over nothing. The smallest frustrations ignited into anger. Then, just as suddenly, they would fall into each other's arms, apologizing with touches rather than words.

Ava wept once, alone in the kitchen after a long day. She wasn't sure if it was exhaustion, or fear, or hunger for her husband's embrace—but she prayed the rosary under her breath, the beads slipping through her fingers like lifelines.

"Dear God," she whispered, "you gave us love. Help us not to lose each other because we're trying too hard to obey."

And so life continued.

The joy of children, the fear of injury, the ache of desire— all wrapped into the everyday holiness of their marriage. In their tiny home, with its patched curtains and uneven floors, Ava and Adam lived the miracle of ordinary sainthood: to love, to suffer, to endure, and to hope.

THE OFFER

Adam receives a life-changing job opportunity in America.

The wind had picked up suddenly, stirring dry leaves and dust into eddies that skittered across the cobbled street. In the distance, thunder growled low and ominous, like some great beast waking from its slumber. Adam, shoulders hunched beneath his work coat, trudged home, the smell of ozone and rain pressing heavily in the air. He was bone-weary, his hands still raw from that morning's climb up a faulty pole in the outer district. He hadn't said anything to Ava, but the near-miss with a live wire had left his heart pounding into the afternoon.

As he turned onto his street, a voice called out from the shadows of a linden tree.

"Adam. Come. We must talk."

It was Joseph.

He stood with a cigarette between his fingers, the glowing ember a lone firefly against the deepening dusk. Adam stepped closer, and Joseph glanced over his shoulder before lowering his voice.

"You look tired, my friend. That job of yours—it's going to kill you one day."

Adam gave a weak shrug. "It's work."

Joseph crushed the cigarette under his boot. "Yes, but there's a storm coming—not just overhead, but in your life. You won't survive many more like today. One bad gust while you're up there and you'll be a ghost before Ava hears the crash."

Adam looked at him, suddenly uneasy. "How do you know what happened?"

"I know more than you think." Joseph's tone shifted, now low and serious. "Which is why I've come to make you an offer. A real one."

He leaned in, eyes sharp. "What if I told you I could get you a visa? Passage to America. A legitimate one. A working paper. A chance."

Adam froze. "That's impossible."

"No. It's expensive," Joseph corrected. "There's a priest I know. He has… let's say 'friends'—one of them high up in the embassy. These things don't move through official channels. It's all very hush-hush. But it's real. A visa in hand, within sixty days."

Adam's heart pounded. "But how much?"

Joseph rubbed his jaw, as though calculating gravity itself. "Because you're young, with a trade and a family, you qualify for a special interest profile. But—and this is important—you own no property, no car, no assets. This makes it harder to prove you'll return home. So, the cost will reflect that risk."

He took a deep breath. "Six thousand greens. Under the table. It covers the priest's coordination, the contact's silence, and—let's be honest—the ambassador's appetite. Nothing moves forward until he's dined, and well."

Adam staggered back a step. "Six thousand? That's more than I earn in a year."

"Yes, but you'll make that in three months in America. Maybe less. Electricians are always needed there. And you're smart. You'll learn fast. But you have to understand—this comes with a price beyond money."

Joseph's voice dropped to a whisper. "You'll have to go alone. For five years. No visits, no letters sent through official channels. If the wrong people ask questions, everything falls apart—for you, for me, for the priest. You can't tell your wife, not yet. When the time comes, you'll explain. Until then, it's silence."

Adam's mouth was dry. "Five years?"

Joseph nodded solemnly. "I know. It's a long time. But what's five years compared to giving your children a future? Compared to coming home with savings, with power, with options?"

He placed a firm hand on Adam's shoulder. "I've seen that look on your face, Adam. The kind of look a man gets when his soul is working overtime and his wallet has nothing to show for it. You're running on hope, and hope needs fuel."

A gust of wind blew between them, bending the linden branches above with a moan like a warning.

"You don't have to decide tonight. But storms like this— they don't always pass quietly. Think about what kind of man you want to be when the skies clear. A survivor… or a casualty."

He turned to go, then paused. "I'll come to you next week. Quietly. If you're ready, we begin. If not… we never speak of it again."

Adam stood there in the rising wind long after Joseph had vanished into the dark. Thunder cracked again in the distance, but inside his chest, the real storm had already begun.

42

THE DECISION

The emotional and spiritual toll of
Adam's decision to leave.

The night Adam came home with the news, the air was tense—heavy, as if the walls of their tiny home could already feel the weight of what was coming.

He waited until the children were asleep and the dinner dishes had been cleared. Then he asked everyone to sit. The single overhead bulb flickered slightly above the kitchen table, casting long shadows over their worried faces.

Ava sensed something was wrong. "What is it?" she asked softly.

Adam exhaled. "Joseph... offered me a way out. A way up. A visa to America."

The words dropped like stones into the silence.

He hesitated, then added, "It will cost six thousand dollars."

Everyone fell still. Even little Margaret, asleep in her crib nearby, seemed to hold her breath.

Momma was the first to speak. Her voice was gentle but filled with anguish. "My son... I love you. I'm proud of the man you are. And I love Ava as if she were my own daughter. But five years... five years without your wife? Without your children?" She looked down, trembling. "What if something happens while you're gone? What if they get sick? What if *you* do?"

Adam reached for her hand. "Even here, bad things happen. But we pray our Rosary every day. We go to Mass. We trust God. And He'll carry us through."

Momma's eyes glistened. "But who will cook for you, clean your clothes, help you survive alone in a place where you don't know the language? Who will be there to warm your heart at night?"

"I will find my way, Momma. I will work, sleep, eat—and pray. Nothing more."

She shook her head, voice breaking. "You are my darling boy. I trust you. But my heart will never stop worrying."

Then Papa spoke. His tone was different—more resolute. "Adam," he said, "you must take this chance. It's a door that may never open again. When I was your age, we had no such possibility. War, poverty, and closed borders made sure of that. But you—you have this moment. Take it. And we will watch over your little brood."

Adam turned toward Ava. Her face was pale, her lips pressed tight.

He could see the storm behind her eyes before she even spoke.

"How can you consider leaving us? The children are so small, just four and five years old. What will they do without their father? What will I do without my husband?"

"I know," Adam whispered. "I know what I'm asking. But this life we're living—it's not enough. We're working ourselves to the bone, rushing between jobs, falling into bed exhausted, snapping at each other. We've lost our laughter, Ava. And I'm scared we'll lose more."

He looked around the small room—the threadbare curtains, the cracked linoleum floor, the creaking cabinets.

"I'm doing this for them—for Daniel and Margaret. So they never have to feel ashamed. So they can go to school, have new clothes, live in a house where the roof doesn't leak. I'm doing this for you. And for Momma and Papa, too. They've given everything."

Ava's voice was barely audible. "You almost died, didn't you?"

He nodded. "Yes. I came close. Closer than I told you. I saw the light flash in front of me. And all I could think of was your face. I can't keep risking my life here for pennies."

Tears rolled down Ava's cheeks. "You can't go. You can't leave me. I need your arms around me at night. I need your lips on my face. I need *you*, Adam."

Adam rushed to her, pulled her close. Momma and Papa followed, embracing her, holding each other in a sacred circle of pain and love.

Papa cleared his throat. "It's decided, then. We will raise the money. Every coin we have saved is yours."

Momma nodded solemnly. "We saved it for retirement, but what good is it if our son breaks his back for nothing? We'll tell the bank it's for building a home."

Ava wiped her tears and said, "My cousin Therese will help. She's offered before. She won't ask questions."

Adam's eyes searched hers. "Are you sure?"

She looked up at him. "No. I'm not sure. I will never be sure. But I believe in you. And I believe in what we're fighting for."

So it began.

That week, Adam's parents emptied their savings. Ava borrowed money from Therese without giving a reason, and

Therese—without asking—simply gave. Still short, Ava made an unthinkable decision: she sold her mother's heirloom china—the same set they used on their wedding day. She also parted with her childhood piano, the one she used to play lullabies on during the quiet nights of their courtship.

As the day of departure drew nearer, the house became a place of long silences and soft touches. The children played, unaware of what was coming.

On the final night, Ava held Adam tightly in their small bedroom.

"Adam," she whispered through her tears, "from the moment I saw you, I belonged to you. I don't know how to live without you beside me. I will ache for you every second you're gone. Every part of me longs for your touch."

He kissed her forehead, her lips, her hands. "I will come back to you. I will work hard and come back as soon as I can. I will call every week, send money without fail. It won't be forever. Just long enough to build our future."

They made love that night—tenderly, reverently, within the quiet boundaries of their Catholic vows, but with a desperation born of looming absence. They held each other afterward in silence, the rise and fall of their breathing the only sound.

Adam lay awake for hours, staring at the ceiling. *Maybe the Catholic calendar method would work this time,* he thought. *But no... they couldn't risk another pregnancy. Not after Margaret. Not now.*

He turned to Ava and kissed her shoulder, already aching for what he hadn't yet lost.

In two months, he would be gone.

He would become what Joseph called a *collector*—gathering not just money, but time, sacrifice, and longing, storing it all in his heart until the day he would finally come home.

FATHER FELIX

*The trusted parish priest whose mentorship
and presence shape many lives.*

The sun was beginning to dip below the horizon, casting long golden beams across the parish grounds as Joseph made his way to the Rosary Garden. He followed the familiar path—worn stones underfoot, the scent of tilled earth and sweet jasmine mingling in the air, undercut by the sharp tang of manure. The garden had become more than a project for Father Felix—it was his sanctuary, his opus, and perhaps his penance.

There he was, as always, hands buried in the dirt, sleeves rolled up, collar slightly askew. Father Felix knelt by a newly planted rosebush, murmuring what could have been a prayer— or a planting mantra. The stone wall behind him, now complete at seven feet high, stood like a fortress of stillness and secrecy, sheltering the faithful from the chaos beyond.

"Father Felix!" Joseph called out.

The priest stood and wiped his hands on a rag tucked into his belt. His face broke into a warm, worn smile.

"Ah, Joseph. Always you find me with soil under my nails and God in my heart."

Joseph's eyes scanned the enclosure. "The men I sent did well. This is more than I imagined. You chose the right two acres. The wall creates a cloistered haven… a perfect space for solitude, for prayer—and for silence."

Father Felix chuckled, brushing dirt from his cassock. "Yes, two acres was wise. Though, I confess, in my heart I longed for three… maybe even five." He laughed and shook his head. "But you saved me from my own excess, thank God."

Joseph took a step closer, his tone shifting. "We have business, Father. One of my thinkers has crossed the line. He's become a collector. Everything is ready."

Father Felix's smile didn't waver, but his eyes sharpened. "Come. Into the office."

The priest's office was a stark contrast to the lush garden and the opulence of the Byzantine-style church. The space was small—ten by twelve, if that—with walls painted a sickly tan color that defied description. A battered wooden desk sat beneath the only window, flanked by chipped filing cabinets and three hard, unwelcoming chairs. Above a modest cupboard hung a simple crucifix, wood worn smooth by decades of quiet reverence.

Joseph placed the envelope on the desk, fat with documents and cash. Six thousand dollars, neatly packed. Father Felix took it without a word, and motioned toward the chair.

"Sit. Let us talk as friends before we speak as… businessmen."

He poured two glasses of whiskey from the bottle he kept hidden in the lower desk drawer—habitual, automatic, as though sacramental. Joseph didn't drink, not during business. He politely declined with a nod.

"Let's do the business," said Father Felix, now all focus.

"Adam. My neighbor. Married, two children."

The priest glanced at the papers and nodded. "Good. A family man. Makes him more believable at the embassy." Then he frowned. "No house. No car. No savings."

"Yes," Joseph said. "That's why I had to raise the price."

Father Felix sipped his whiskey thoughtfully. "Then it's settled. I'll go to the embassy. Make the introductions. They'll expect... gifts. Nothing happens without ceremony."

He opened the envelope and counted the bills with care, eyes briefly narrowing in satisfaction. Then, without pause, he slid five hundred back across the desk to Joseph, who pocketed it silently.

"Tell me, Joseph—did you see the trumpet vines on the garden wall? And the ivy? God willing, the high privet hedges will soon enclose the three prayer circles. And in each alcove, I've planned a pond—yes, a pond! With koi fish and floating lilies. It will be a marvel."

He smiled, drifting into the vision that lived in his soul.

"I thank heaven I studied agriculture before entering seminary. Who knew it would serve Our Lady's Garden so well? Statues, plaques, benches… it will all be in place by winter."

Joseph waited for the reverie to fade before speaking. "I have two more thinkers and another collector warming up. There will be more customers."

Father Felix raised his glass. "To them. May they water the Garden of the Mother of God."

Joseph stood, declining the toast. "Another time, Father. I've other business today."

The priest downed both drinks without hesitation, then wiped his mouth and stood.

"Bring me more customers. This year must be abundant. I must complete the garden before the snow."

"I will. But remember, tomorrow the contractors begin work on the Grotto of the Immaculate. Keep them happy—but not too happy."

Father Felix grinned and reached under his desk, lifting a large bottle of vodka. "For after work only. I've saved this for them."

Joseph raised an eyebrow. "Only one bottle, Father?"

"I have one for them," the priest said, eyes twinkling. "The rest are for me."

They both laughed—though Joseph's laugh was brief and hollow.

"God bless you, Father."

"God bless you, my son."

As Joseph turned to leave, Father Felix lingered at the window, watching the last light fade over his unfinished Rosary Garden. In the distance, the trees swayed, whispering secrets in the dusk wind.

The garden was growing. So was the price of its beauty.

And beneath the sacred soil, something darker had begun to take root.

DEPARTURE

*A painful goodbye as Adam leaves for a
future of promise and separation.*

The morning of Adam's departure arrived like a heavy shroud draped over the household. The sky was gunmetal gray, the air still and tense, as if nature itself were holding its breath. The children, still groggy from sleep, clung to their mother's legs, confused and uneasy. They didn't understand the magnitude of what was happening—only that something was being taken from them.

Joseph arrived promptly, his car idling at the curb like an unspoken countdown. Inside, Ava moved mechanically, folding Adam's last shirt, adjusting the strap on his duffel bag, her fingers trembling. Momma stood at the stove pretending to stir soup that wasn't there, while Papa paced near the doorway, eyes darting between the clock and the front window.

Adam kneeled and embraced Daniel and little Margaret, holding them so tightly they squealed, unsure whether to laugh or cry. He whispered promises into their ears—of toys and stories and a house with a garden—things he hoped he could make true. Then he looked into their eyes one last time, drinking in every freckle, every curl, every breath.

When it came time to go, he turned to Ava. She had not cried. Not once. Her face was an exquisite mask of control. But her silence cut deeper than any weeping. It was the silence of someone floating outside herself, as if watching the whole moment unfold from a corner of the ceiling. She felt weightless. Numb. The way she had felt when she was told her parents had died. As if the world had dropped out from under her and she was suspended in air, untethered, watching her husband—her life—walk out the door.

Joseph placed a hand on Adam's shoulder. "It's time," he said quietly. "We can't be late."

Adam hesitated for a heartbeat longer. He bent down again, kissing each child, breathing in their warmth. Then, with one last look at Ava, he turned, walked out, and did not look back.

The airport was chaos incarnate. Screaming infants, anxious travelers, flashing monitors, guards barking orders. The cacophony did nothing to ease the strain in Adam's chest. He kept glancing behind him, trying to hold onto the faces of Ava, Momma, and Papa—each expression seared into his memory with painful clarity. Ava's lips had trembled, but she had said nothing. Momma had pressed a rosary into his hand. Papa had simply nodded, his eyes glassy with pride and fear.

The security line was long and slow. Adam clutched his small bag and pressed the rosary to his lips, murmuring a prayer in his native tongue. When he finally passed through the checkpoint, it felt like a door slamming shut behind him. He was alone now. Entirely alone.

The airplane was cramped, the air recycled and dry. The other passengers were wedged in like cargo—shoulder to shoulder, knees against the seat in front. The smell of body heat and jet fuel hung in the air. As the engines roared to life and the plane hurtled down the runway, Adam gripped the armrests tightly, his palms slick with sweat.

Then they were in the air—ascending, rising above the gray, into a tapestry of clouds bathed in golden light. Through the window, the ground shrank away, until villages became dots, roads became threads, and eventually, only the sky remained.

He leaned his head against the window, watching the world fall away. There were clouds like mountains, some glowing with sunlight, others bruised with thunder. A flash of lightning streaked through the distance—raw and magnificent. And then, to the east, a pale rainbow unfurled across the heavens like a promise.

"God is awesome," Adam whispered to himself, awe and fear mingling in his chest.

Hours passed. Somewhere over the Atlantic, a stewardess handed him a steaming tray. The food, though ordinary, felt sacred. He hadn't realized how hungry he was. He ate slowly, savoring each bite. The coffee that followed was dark and rich, cutting through the exhaustion that had weighed on him all day.

For the first time in hours, he allowed his body to relax. The knot in his stomach loosened. The worry, the anticipation, the impossible goodbye—they were still there, but dulled now by fatigue and distance.

He closed his eyes and drifted into sleep.

He dreamt of Ava.

Her eyes, wide and glistening.

Her laughter, like silver bells.

The soft weight of her in his arms, the way she whispered his name in the quiet hours of the night.

But in the dream, she was always just out of reach.

A voice broke through the haze of sleep.

"Ladies and gentlemen, we are now preparing to land. Please fasten your seatbelts."

Adam startled awake. For a moment, he didn't know where he was. Then it all came rushing back.

He checked his jacket pocket—his passport was there. He touched it like a lifeline.

Looking out the window again, he saw land. Vast, unfamiliar. A new world.

His future.

His exile.

His hope.

His sacrifice.

And there, in the distance, the plane began its slow descent into America.

ARRIVAL TO THE USA

*Adam faces the reality of immigrant
life and economic pressure.*

The moment Adam stepped into the vast international terminal of Chicago's O'Hare Airport, he was swept into a whirlwind of sensation. The air was thick with unfamiliar smells—burnt coffee, floor polish, perfume, sweat, and something industrial that he couldn't name. The buzz of voices filled the space like a hive, but it wasn't just one language—it was dozens. German, French, Chinese, Spanish, Arabic, English. All around him were people of every shape and shade, some dressed in sleek modern suits, others in brilliant traditional garments that shimmered under the terminal lights.

He stood there, rooted in place, a single figure amid the constant motion. The automatic announcements blared overhead—"Please do not leave your baggage unattended"— and still, Adam didn't move. He was trying to take it all in: the clean brightness of the ceiling lights, the massive glass windows, the advertisements in bold neon, the speed at which everything and everyone seemed to move. This place didn't walk—it surged.

Someone tapped him on the shoulder.

"Hey there, are you Adam?"

He turned quickly. "Yes… I am. You must be Paul?"

"That's me. Welcome to America, brother." Paul offered a wide smile and a firm handshake. He was tall—almost comically so—with long limbs and a narrow face. His nose arched prominently, but his warm eyes put Adam immediately at ease.

"How was the flight?" Paul asked as he grabbed one of Adam's bags.

Adam smiled faintly, still dazed. "It was exhilarating. A little frightening at first. But once in the air—it was like flying into God's own sky."

Paul chuckled. "Come on. Let's get you settled. You'll feel human again once you've had a meal and some sleep."

They exited the terminal into the chilled Chicago air. The wind bit through Adam's coat, but he hardly noticed. His eyes were wide as he followed Paul to a sleek, gleaming car parked outside.

Adam ran a hand over the hood, awestruck. "What kind of car is this?"

"Cadillac STS. American-made luxury," Paul said proudly, unlocking it.

Adam slid into the plush beige leather seat like a man entering a dream. "It's like sitting inside a cloud."

The car rumbled to life and they merged into the flood of traffic. Adam stared, speechless, at the towering skyline, the endless web of freeways, the blinking signs, and storefronts full of everything he had only seen in old magazines. It was like a living machine—pulsing, grinding, surging forward.

"This city…" Adam whispered. "It's like an anthill… but made of steel."

Paul laughed. "Pretty much."

They drove for nearly an hour until they reached a quiet neighborhood of red brick homes. One of them stood larger than the others, with ornate trim and wide front steps.

"You'll be staying here," Paul said. "In the basement apartment. It's clean, warm, and private enough. You'll share with three other guys. We all started this way. Joseph makes sure we're treated well."

Adam's mouth parted slightly. "This is… where I live now?"

"Yes. And you'll have two full days to rest. On the third day, you begin work."

"Work? Already?" Adam said, surprised but eager. "What kind of job?"

"You'll be at a warehouse. Electrical supplies. Some of it you'll know already, and the rest you'll pick up fast."

Adam nodded, grateful. "I can't wait to tell my family. They'll be proud."

Paul reached into the glove compartment and handed him a prepaid phone card. "Here's your first one. I'll show you how to use it, but after this you'll need to buy them yourself. Come on. Let's get you settled, then you can call Ava."

The basement apartment was much more than Adam had expected. The walls were paneled in rich oak, the carpet was soft and freshly vacuumed. The shared space was orderly and smelled faintly of detergent. His personal room had a single bed with wool blankets, a small desk, and a dresser. It was modest, but it was warm, private, and safe. He was impressed.

Before unpacking, Paul guided him to the phone in the kitchen and dialed out for him. Adam clutched the receiver, waiting. The second he heard her voice, he nearly wept.

"Ava? My love—it's me. I've arrived. I'm here."

There was a pause. "Adam? Oh… thank God. I've missed you terribly."

He could hear the strain in her voice, the tightness behind her words. She was holding herself together for the sake of the children.

"I'm safe, I promise. The plane ride was long but beautiful. I looked out the window and saw the world fall away. You would have loved it, Ava. I wish you were with me."

"How is the place where you'll stay?"

"It's warm. Clean. I share it, but I have my own bed and dresser. And Ava… I have a job. Already."

"You what?" she asked, surprised.

Adam chuckled. "Warehouse work. Electrical supplies. I start in two days."

He told her about the Cadillac, the apartment, the bustle of Chicago. Then he told her the best part.

"They'll pay me three hundred fifty dollars a week. And I'll only pay fifty for rent."

Ava gasped. "That's more than we've ever had at one time… You'll send it back?"

"Every week. I promise."

There was silence, then: "I'm proud of you. I hate that you're there… and not here. But I'm proud."

They exchanged words of love—quiet, trembling, real. When he hung up, Adam leaned against the wall and closed his eyes. Her voice had anchored him. For the first time since landing, he felt truly at peace.

That night, he unpacked his small suitcase. Folded his few shirts. Placed the rosary from his mother on the nightstand. Then he slipped under the warm blankets and flipped the light off. The room fell into darkness, a soft hush pressing in around him.

He whispered a prayer.

Then he closed his eyes and dreamed—not of skyscrapers or Cadillac cars—but of Ava's smile and the soft weight of his daughter in his arms.

Tomorrow, a new life would begin.

And he would make it count.

JOB

*Adam's struggle and perseverance
in the labor market.*

On a cold Monday morning, Adam stood at the corner of a bustling Chicago street, gripping the steel pole of the CTA bus stop as wind whipped through his coat. The sky above was a dull pewter gray, and the buildings loomed like giants lost in fog. The city felt cold—impersonal—but alive, pulsing with opportunity and challenge. When the bus arrived, he stepped on with determination, clutching a slip of paper where Paul had scribbled directions to the warehouse.

He found a seat and stared out the window, watching the neighborhoods pass—brick houses, corner stores, people walking dogs or sipping coffee on their porches. In his pocket, his fingers brushed the small rosary his mother had given him. "For strength," she had said through tears. Now, he needed it more than ever.

The warehouse was massive—far larger than anything he had seen back home. A steel building stretched out like an airplane hangar, filled with shelves stacked ten feet high, loaded with spools of wiring, outlets, breakers, fixtures, tools, transformers, and more things he couldn't yet name. The air inside smelled of sawdust, dust, and metal. Machines whirred in the background, and the murmur of workers echoed like distant thunder.

A stocky supervisor named Mick gave Adam a brisk tour and rattled off instructions with a heavy Midwestern accent. Adam caught every other word but nodded respectfully, watching closely and mimicking what he saw. His job was to receive, sort, and restock electrical components. At first glance, it felt familiar—this was his world, after all—but on a scale that stunned him.

He was surrounded by men who moved with practiced indifference. Some glanced at him curiously; others looked away, uninterested or worse—hostile. A few muttered behind his back, not bothering to hide the resentment.

"Another one of them," he overheard one man grumble. "Always smiling, always trying to impress."

But Adam didn't let it faze him. He worked hard—harder than he ever had—ten hours a day, sometimes more, lifting, labeling, logging, learning. His hands ached, his back burned, and by the end of each shift, his muscles felt as though they'd been hammered. But he was grateful. Every aching bone reminded him of why he was here: for Ava, for Daniel and Margaret, for Momma and Papa.

Some of the workers softened. A Latino man named Luis noticed Adam's quiet persistence and began pointing out tools and terms in English and Spanish.

"Breaker panel," Luis said one day, tapping a heavy gray box. "Panel de interruptores."

"Breaker panel," Adam repeated, grateful. "Gracias."

"You learn fast," Luis nodded.

During lunch breaks, Adam practiced his English with his roommates. In the evenings, he scribbled new words into a notebook, sounding them out phonetically until they felt familiar on his tongue. It was slow work, but he improved quickly. He loved the language—not just the words, but the way Americans used them with such casual humor and rhythm.

Each morning before sunrise, he walked two blocks to a small Catholic church tucked between a diner and a pharmacy. It was a modest building, but beautiful in its simplicity. There, in the quiet glow of candlelight, he knelt before the tabernacle and offered his exhaustion and his hopes. The Mass was said in English, but the prayers were the same. The Rosary felt like home.

Every Sunday, Adam called his family. Paul had helped him get a second-hand flip phone, and with a new calling card each week, he rang home like clockwork.

"Momma, Papa… how are you?"

"Daniel! Did you behave this week?"

"Margaret, my princess, are you walking more now?"

And finally, "Ava… my love. I miss you. Every hour, every breath."

Ava's voice came through the line like music he hadn't heard in years. Sometimes she sounded strong and playful, teasing him. Other times, her voice trembled with fatigue and longing. But always, she ended the call with three words he needed to hear more than air: *"I love you."*

The ache of their separation lived constantly beneath his ribs. His arms ached not just from lifting crates, but from the absence of holding her. At night, in the silence of his small room, he thought of her. Not just her laughter or her voice, but the feel of her in his arms, the way her breath slowed when she fell asleep beside him, the way she fit against his body like a missing piece of his soul.

Other men in the apartment bragged of girls they met at bars or nightclubs. One even offered to "set him up."

Adam smiled politely, then turned away.

His body may have been lonely, but his heart was full—and faithful.

AVA'S DEBTS

*Back home, Ava manages finances
and rising burdens alone.*

Six months had passed since Adam boarded that plane and left a piece of himself behind. In his absence, Ava had become both mother and father, daughter and provider—a quiet pillar of strength wrapped in soft-spoken resilience.

Each week, without fail, Adam sent money home. The crisp, foreign bills arrived like lifelines, handwritten notes tucked in with the remittance, each one filled with longing and promises: *"Soon, my love. Soon we will be together again."*

With fierce discipline, Ava repaid every debt. The loan from Therese, the silent sacrifice of Momma and Papa's retirement fund, the sale of her mother's heirlooms—each was honored. Piece by piece, she was reclaiming their dignity.

Though she worked part time at the preschool, Ava managed the home like a seasoned general—scheduling every hour, saving every coin. But she noticed Momma moving slower, wincing at times when she thought no one was looking.

"Mamma, it's time," Ava said one morning, gently placing her hand over hers at the breakfast table. "Let me carry the load now. You've done more than enough."

Momma laughed softly, brushing it off. "I'm not an old woman yet."

"You are a wonder," Ava smiled. "But even wonders must rest."

Papa agreed. "We need you whole. Not broken from pride." That settled it.

Momma finally retired and found new joy in her kitchen—baking, preserving, passing down recipes with flour-covered hands and stories that smelled of cinnamon and memory. Ava took on the heavier chores, her body growing stronger even as her heart remained tender.

By month seven, a miracle arrived: Ava had saved enough to buy a car—a small, cherry-red hatchback that gleamed like hope on wheels. When Papa exited the factory that evening, sweaty and tired from his shift, he stopped in his tracks at the sound of familiar voices.

"Papa! Papa!"

There they were—Ava, Daniel, and Margaret waving from the curb. Even Momma clapped from the front seat.

His jaw dropped, then split into a grin so wide and boyish that Ava's eyes welled with tears. *This*—this joy, this pride—was the reward for every sleepless night, every ache and sacrifice. That look on Papa's face was something she would carry in her heart forever.

Empowered by the progress they had made, Ava began to think ahead. *They needed a home—something of their own.* Not a rental, not borrowed space—but land, soil they could claim, where Adam's dreams could take root and grow.

She searched for weeks before stumbling upon it—two acres nestled at the edge of a quiet village. A winding stream curled through the property like a silver ribbon. Towering trees stood like guardians, their leaves whispering in the breeze. In spring, wildflowers bloomed in joyful abandon. In autumn, the canopy exploded in crimson, amber, and gold.

Standing in the middle of that land, Ava felt something stir inside her—a sacred knowing. *This was the place.*

She knelt down, scooped a handful of earth, and let it crumble between her fingers. It was rich, dark, and smelled of rain and promise. She pictured a house with wide porches, the sound of children laughing, the smell of fresh bread wafting from the kitchen. A garden to rival Eden, tended by her and Momma. Trees where Daniel and Margaret could climb and dream.

But dreams needed structure—and she knew she couldn't do it alone.

She would go to Joseph. He had helped Adam. He knew the land, the builders, the costs, the permits, the hidden pitfalls. She needed his wisdom to make the right decision.

Still kneeling, Ava closed her eyes and whispered, "Lord, if this is the place, open the doors. Let this ground be the foundation for our future, the soil of our joy."

The wind blew gently through the trees, and for a moment, it felt like Adam's arms were wrapped around her, whispering in her ear, *"I'm still with you."*

PROMOTIONS

Adam's rise through hard work,
offering a glimpse of hope.

Adam had always believed in quiet perseverance, but even he was stunned when opportunity came knocking with a full stride. It had been nearly a year since he'd arrived in America, and now, the tides were turning.

Mr. Madden, the stern but fair contractor Adam had been working under for several months, called him into his office on a bright spring morning. The air smelled of fresh-cut wood and rain, and the sunlight filtered through the cracked blinds like golden confetti. Adam wiped his hands on his jeans and entered, his heart beating a little faster.

Mr. Madden handed him a crisp envelope. Inside were documents certifying Adam as a qualified electrician. Adam's breath caught in his throat.

"You're a hard worker," Mr. Madden said, gruffly but not unkindly. "You've earned this. Report to Jake. You're joining the electrical team—starting next Monday. Pay's doubled. One thousand a week."

Adam stood frozen, as if his feet were cemented to the concrete floor. The words "one thousand dollars a week" echoed in his ears. He thought of Ava, of Daniel and Margaret. He thought of the land she'd found—the one with the stream that ran like a silver vein through the trees—and his heart soared. *Now it could be real. Now we can begin to build.*

That night, when he called home, his voice trembled with excitement.

"Ava… we can build the house."

She gasped, covering her mouth with her hand. Her voice, soft and fragile, cracked like a glass ornament dropped from too high: "You really think so?"

"Yes. It's happening, my love. I can see it now."

But for all the good news, their separation still carved into Ava like winter wind. Many nights, after the children had gone to sleep, she would sit in the dark and cry—alone, abandoned in the stillness of their marriage bed. Her only comfort was the thought that they would *soon* be together. She whispered it like a prayer, over and over, as if repetition could make it real: "Soon… soon… we'll all be together again."

Adam missed her with a physical ache, a hollow throb in his chest and loins. He never looked at another woman. Not once. His devotion to Ava was unshakable, though the loneliness was suffocating.

To pass the time and make the most of his days, Adam attended morning Mass every day before work. The church's flickering candles and holy silence soothed him. He now knew enough English to go to confession, to speak to strangers in the pews, and to read scriptures aloud without stumbling.

He had moved out of the basement and into a proper first-floor apartment with four other men. The apartment was large—three bedrooms, two baths—and close to both the CTA and METRA lines. But it wasn't a home. The other men were kind, but their lives were ruled by beer, women, and laziness. Empty cans littered the kitchen, half-eaten takeout crusted the counters, and the bathroom was a swamp of disregard. Adam tolerated it—up to a point. Eventually, he cleaned the bathroom himself and told them, "If you want a maid, you pay me." They laughed, but some gave him money.

He kept to himself. Their chaos was not his.

Instead, he found moments of joy outdoors. At lunch, he would sit on a bench in the sun, eat his sandwich slowly, and watch birds build their nests in the crevices of the building. On weekends, he often walked to the edge of Lake Michigan. The vast, glittering water reminded him of home, and he liked to watch the gulls swoop down to catch fish or steal bread crumbs from careless hands. The lake smelled clean—briny, alive—and it spoke to a part of him that nothing else could reach.

Then, one Sunday afternoon, a new kind of miracle arrived.

He had sent Ava a computer with a webcam—his biggest purchase yet—and now, for the first time since his departure, he could *see* her. Her face lit up the screen like the moon on a cloudless night. He saw the children, their cheeks fuller, their eyes sparkling. It was heaven, and it was agony. To see them was a gift—but not being able to touch them, hold them, kiss their soft skin—it was a fresh wound.

"Daddy…! Papa and I went fishing and I caught a big fish!" Daniel shouted, his little voice piercing through the static like sunlight through blinds. "Momma cooked it, even Margaret liked it!"

Adam laughed, his chest swelling. "That's exactly what Papa and I did when I was your age. Next time, you take her too. And maybe… I'll catch one here and show you."

Inspired, Adam walked into a local tackle shop that weekend. The owner—a wiry old man with a crooked smile—recommended worms for perch and spoons for salmon. "Get yourself a net, too," he advised. "You'll need it."

Adam started small. Perch. Less expensive, easier to catch. The following weekend, he stood on the break wall by the marina, casting into the gray-blue water. He caught eight hand-sized perch and walked home with a proud grin. He cooked them the way his mother taught him—lightly floured, pan-fried in oil, a squeeze of lemon. That night, he slept with a full stomach and a fuller heart.

But joy was still laced with sorrow. Another summer was coming, and he remained apart from the ones he loved. The ache never left. He often asked himself, *Have I chosen the right path? Is this price too high for the dream we're chasing?*

Then came Sunday Mass, and Father Jensen's homily rang through the air like a hammer on iron:

"Money does not buy happiness. You cannot purchase peace or joy in any store. True happiness comes from giving—especially to those who can give you nothing in return."

That same week, the 2004 earthquake and tsunami struck. Adam watched the devastation on television—ruined villages, crying mothers, children clinging to debris. It shattered something inside him.

He called Ava. "I want to send something—to help them. Just a little. Maybe a hundred?"

"Yes," she said without hesitation. "Do it. We have more than enough."

And so he did.

That night, Adam lit a candle and whispered a prayer in the dark.

"Lord, I'm not whole without them. But if I can give even a piece of myself to help another, let that piece be enough—for now."

DANIEL'S FIRST COMMUNION

*A proud, bittersweet moment for Ava
without Adam by her side.*

A crisp spring breeze swept through the countryside as Ava pulled the little red car onto a winding gravel path, her heart fluttering with anticipation. Mamma, Papa, and the children were all with her, their faces pressed to the windows as the land she had long dreamed of owning finally came into view.

The two-acre plot rolled out before them like a promise—untamed, beautiful, waiting. A gentle stream whispered through a wooded hollow, and the trees, just beginning to bud with green, rustled softly in the breeze.

"Look, children!" Papa pointed as he stepped out of the car, his gait slightly slower than before. "There's a stream in the woods—come! Let's see if there are fish in it."

The children giggled and ran toward the water, their joy bouncing in the air like birdsong.

Mamma's eyes sparkled as she took in the land. "Oh, Ava… Adam will be *so* proud when he comes home." Her voice trembled slightly, carried off by the breeze before she could finish her thought.

Ava reached for her hand and kissed her cheek gently. "He *will* come home, Mamma. Very soon." The words escaped her lips with forced brightness, but in her chest they rang hollow. She repeated them like a chant to herself sometimes—praying they would eventually feel true.

That Sunday at Mass, a new presence stirred the parish. Pastor Thomas stepped up to the pulpit with a proud smile.

"Dear parishioners, it is my pleasure to introduce our new Associate Pastor, Father Mark."

A hush fell over the congregation as Father Mark ascended the altar. He was strikingly tall and lean, with jet-black hair swept neatly from his forehead and penetrating dark eyes. His cassock was immaculate, his demeanor elegant—almost theatrical. The air in the church shifted as eyes—especially the women's—followed his every move. Whispers bloomed like wildflowers in pews. *So handsome… so young… how lucky we are.*

After Mass, Ava and her children approached to greet the new priest. Daniel and Margaret clutched her skirt, wide-eyed with curiosity.

Father Mark knelt slightly and spoke kindly to the children, his voice warm and controlled. When he stood, his collar had slipped slightly from place. Without thinking, Ava reached up and gently tucked it back in.

"Congratulations, Father," she said, smiling. "This is a good parish, and you're in good hands."

As her fingers brushed his collar, a strange chill ran through her. She composed herself quickly. "My son Daniel will be making his First Communion next spring. I've been asked to be the chairperson for all the events and purchases."

Father Mark's smile widened, but Ava noticed something strange—his eyes remained unreadable, like still water with hidden depths. "Ah, I'll be teaching the children," he said smoothly. "Confession and Holy Communion. And I'll handle their final rehearsals. It will be an honor."

He watched her closely as she spoke, storing away every detail about her husband working abroad, the money being sent, and the house being built. What Ava shared freely out of warmth, Father Mark absorbed with the cool calculation of a man who measured every opportunity.

As spring bloomed into May, the parish was abuzz with preparations for First Communion. Lace veils and white suits filled closets. Volunteers arranged flowers, baked cookies, and ironed linens. Father Mark led the children through catechism with theatrical reverence—his voice low and hypnotic, his gaze always flickering toward Ava when she wasn't looking.

The day of the First Communion arrived bathed in golden sunlight. The church gleamed—polished pews, glowing candles, the altar adorned with lilies and violets. The children filed in, hands folded, solemn and radiant in their ceremonial attire. Parents clutched tissues. Grandparents wept softly.

Therese and Dora flanked Ava as she wiped a proud tear watching Daniel process down the aisle.

"Papa will be proud," Therese whispered.

Ava nodded, her eyes never leaving her son.

After the ceremony, the children presented Father Mark with a bouquet of white roses and the parents gathered to offer a gift—a large envelope filled with donations.

Ava approached last, holding out her own envelope with a shy smile. "Thank you, Father, for all you've done. The children will remember this day forever. And so will we."

His hand brushed hers as he accepted the envelope. "The pleasure has been mine," he said. His lips smiled, but again, not his eyes.

Later, in his private rectory room, Father Mark opened the envelopes alone. His fingers paused as he reached Ava's. Inside was five hundred dollars in crisp bills. A satisfied grin curled across his face.

This woman is loyal… generous… and her husband is far away. This parish is a gift from Heaven.

Weeks passed, and the weather grew warmer. One Sunday afternoon, Father Mark was invited to bless the land Ava and Adam had purchased.

He walked the soil solemnly, murmuring prayers as Ava, Mamma, and Papa followed behind him with folded hands. The stream gurgled beside them. When the prayer ended, Ava handed him another envelope.

He didn't open it there, but felt the weight. Another five hundred.

As he tucked it into his robes, he said with a soft smile, "Would we go for lunch before returning?"

Ava hesitated. "Oh, that would be lovely, Father, but I must take Papa to the doctor. His chest has been tight lately. This last cold hasn't let him go."

Father Mark nodded, appearing concerned. "Of course. I'll pray for him. I'm sure the doctor will know what to do."

"But perhaps," Ava added, almost apologetically, "you could come for dinner instead? We'll have more time to talk once the day is done."

Father Mark's eyes glinted. "Ah… yes. A much better initiative," he said, his voice honeyed. "Dinner will give us… time for a more remarkable conversation."

Ava smiled politely, not noticing the weight of his stare as she turned away—already gathering the children and calling out to Papa. But Father Mark remained where he was for a moment, staring at the trees and the land before him, his mind calculating.

Yes. Very remarkable indeed.

AVA AND FATHER MARK

An evolving relationship of trust,
vulnerability, and moral complexity.

The candles flickered softly in the dining room of Adam's parents' modest but well-kept home. The scent of roasted lamb and rosemary filled the air. Ava moved gracefully between the kitchen and the table, refilling glasses, checking on Mamma's needs, and gently nudging Margaret to eat her vegetables. Papa's quiet cough punctuated the occasional lull in conversation. And at the head of the table, comfortable and assured, sat Father Mark.

He had become a frequent guest now. What started as occasional visits for parish planning had evolved into regular meals and shared errands. Somehow, he had inserted himself into their lives with grace and ease—his presence now felt expected, even welcomed.

"Margaret will be preparing for her First Holy Communion soon," Father Mark announced between bites, glancing down the table toward the little girl, who beamed with pride. "And I propose, if everyone agrees, that Ava once again take charge of the ceremony arrangements."

He turned to Ava with a soft, approving smile. "Your work last year was flawless. The parents still talk about it."

Ava's cheeks flushed, both from the compliment and from the growing unease she felt under Father Mark's attentive gaze. Mamma and Papa nodded enthusiastically.

"She is the only one who knows how to make everything look like Heaven on Earth," Mamma said with a wink.

"Do you think the other parents will agree?" Ava asked, trying to sound composed.

"Of course," Father Mark said smoothly. "They remember the beauty, the precision… and the generosity. There will be no objections."

And just like that, Ava found herself once again chairing the First Communion preparations—ordering altar flowers, organizing parents, coordinating children's garments and music. The work consumed her days, and for a while, she was grateful. It kept her distracted from darker thoughts, from the creeping loneliness, from the weight of her growing doubts.

Though Adam's weekly phone calls continued, they felt thinner somehow, as if time and distance were stripping the warmth from his voice. Ava would cradle the receiver and listen to his stories of work, of weather, of far-off Chicago winds, and feel the ache grow deeper in her chest. He spoke often of sending more money. But never of coming home.

Does he still dream of me the way I dream of him? Has someone taken my place in his bed, even just for comfort?

The thoughts stabbed her like needles, unwelcome and yet impossible to silence.

And in the quiet of her own body, desire stirred. There were nights—lonely, cold nights—when her longing consumed her.

The heat of memory, the press of Adam's body, his breath on her skin... it haunted her like a ghost. But no matter how her body cried out, she knew she could never give herself to another man. She belonged to Adam, and always would.

Still, there was a hunger inside her she could no longer ignore.

One day, while hanging damp linens in the backyard, the weight of everything—the separation, the responsibility, the wondering—came crashing down. The sun was high, the sheets crisp with the scent of lavender, and yet her knees buckled slightly. The clothespin dropped from her hand, and before she knew it, tears were pouring down her cheeks.

She wept openly, silently, letting the laundry flutter around her like sails in a wind she couldn't control. Her hands clutched the sheet like it was a lifeline, her face buried in cotton, muffling her sobs.

Come home, Adam. Please come home.

Later that week, Father Mark arrived to drop off new catechism materials. He caught Ava in the garden, her hair tied back, sleeves rolled up, dirt under her fingernails. Her eyes were still red from the earlier cry, though she smiled when she saw him.

He stepped closer than he needed to. "You've been working hard. Everything you touch turns to beauty, Ava."

She looked down, flustered. "It's just a garden. Mamma helps me."

Father Mark's gaze lingered too long. "Still, it blossoms under your care."

He offered to help move a heavy planter box, and she nodded, grateful for the help. But when their hands touched around the wooden frame, the air between them shifted—charged, tense.

Ava quickly let go and stepped back. "I should go check on Papa. He's resting."

"Of course," he said, smoothly masking his disappointment. "Will I see you tomorrow? There's a planning meeting after Mass."

"Yes," she replied quickly, turning to go.

As she walked away, she could feel his eyes on her back. Not the gaze of a shepherd watching his flock—but of a man watching a flame he wished he could touch.

Inside the house, Ava closed the door behind her and exhaled sharply. She didn't know what frightened her more— the intensity in Father Mark's eyes, or the flicker of curiosity it sparked in her.

But one thing she did know.

She missed her husband with every breath she took.

ADAM'S LIFE

*A parallel portrait of Adam's emotional
and moral descent in the U.S.*

Adam's days passed in a blur of sweat, steel, and silence. He worked tirelessly—twelve-hour shifts in the brutal heat of summer and the biting winds of winter. His hands were calloused, his back ached constantly, and his shoulders carried more than the weight of tools—they bore the burden of a family left behind. Yet Adam never complained. Each long hour was a brick in the foundation he was laying for their future. Each dollar earned was a step closer to the life they had dreamed of.

Evenings were quieter now. He lived in a small second-floor apartment with two other laborers who kept to themselves. It wasn't home, not really. But it was warm, quiet, and clean—enough for a man with no time for distractions. Most nights, Adam sat by the window with a bowl of rice and vegetables, watching the light dim across the city. The skyline was impressive, yes—but it held no magic for him. His eyes were always fixed eastward, toward the place where the sun would rise on his family.

Every week, Ava sent him photos in the mail—Daniel smiling, now tall and lanky like a sapling stretching to the sky; Margaret in her First Communion dress, glowing like a pearl in sunlight. The images pierced his heart. He traced their faces with his fingers, memorizing every detail.

Daniel is nine already...

I've missed so much. When I left, he was five. Margaret was just four...

That realization hit him like a punch to the chest. A lifetime of moments lost—first bike rides, missing teeth, bedtime stories he couldn't read aloud. And now Margaret would make her First Holy Communion… and he would not be there.

It was this gnawing ache that he brought with him to Sunday Mass at St. Peter's. The church was modest, but Father Jensen's words always seemed to find him where he most needed to be found.

This Sunday, the homily cut deep:

"Sometimes, life calls us far from home—through war, through work, through tragedy. But even in distance, we are not released from our vows.

Faithfulness is not simply about resisting temptation. It is about staying emotionally present.

Adultery is not just an act—it is the slow forgetting of love, the turning away from our families in small, silent ways.

We must fight to remember them. We must fight to feel them."

Adam bowed his head and wept silently in the pew. He hadn't been unfaithful to Ava—not in body. But his heart? His mind? He couldn't deny that something had started to fade. He was terrified by how easily the days passed now without him hearing her voice. The truth of it clawed at him—his memory of her face, her laughter, even the way she said his name—was blurring around the edges.

How did this happen? When did she become a memory instead of a presence?

I can't let this happen. I can't lose her.

He considered bringing it up during their weekly phone call, but how? How do you confess to your wife that she feels like a dream slipping from your fingers?

That night, he lay in bed fully clothed, the latest photo of Ava and the children pressed against his chest like a relic. He drifted into sleep with their faces in his mind, and dreamed—not of the church, not of work, not of America—but of Ava. In his dream, she was beside him again, laughing in the garden, her hair blowing in the wind, her body warm and close. He reached for her. He kissed her. He made love to her with an urgency that only distance could ignite.

Then he woke up to cold sheets and silence.

Alone.

He stared at the ceiling until dawn, feeling a hollow ache that no money could fill.

He remembered another homily—months ago—about helping the poor. He had felt moved, convicted. That week, he had donated one hundred dollars to earthquake victims on the other side of the world. Later, he read in a newspaper that only one cent of each dollar had reached the people in need. Betrayed by the system, he vowed never again.

From then on, everything he gave went directly to his own—clothing for Papa, medicine for Mamma, a computer for the children, shoes, toys, books, packages of dried goods, tools, kitchen equipment, and money—always money. It was his way of staying present, of showing his love when his arms could not.

But even that began to feel like a thin thread. It was not the same as his voice reading bedtime stories. It was not the same as the warmth of his body next to Ava's under the soft folds of their shared blanket.

He prayed constantly—not for riches, not for more work—but for the grace to keep his family's love alive across the miles. That the memory of him would not fade from his children's hearts. That Ava would not stop waiting for him.

Let them know I am coming back. Let them still want me when I do.

Adam looked up at the dark sky beyond the window, and for the first time in a long time, whispered out loud:

"God… bring me home."

MARGARET'S FIRST COMMUNION

Another sacred moment in Ava's spiritual journey.

The preparations for Margaret's First Communion swept Ava into a familiar rhythm—meetings, purchases, fittings, and rehearsals—all coordinated with the precision of someone who had done it once before. Yet this year felt heavier. Not because of the work, but because of the absence she could no longer ignore.

Ava and Father Mark met often—sometimes under the formal cover of parish business, sometimes simply because it had become convenient. A brief meal after selecting veils and missals… a shared coffee while discussing donations… a ride offered when her little red car had trouble starting.

He had a way of making her feel important—heard. As if every word she spoke was worthy of attention. Ava told herself this was what priests did: they listened, they served, they consoled. And yet, she couldn't deny that she was more careful with her appearance when she knew she'd be seeing him.

Wherever they went, Father Mark turned heads. He was magnetic, with his tailored Roman collar and flowing black cassock, which never had a wrinkle. His cologne was subtle but lingering—something expensive. His shoes, clearly Italian, never bore the scuffs of hard wear. People greeted him with reverence, even awe. They whispered that they were lucky—**blessed**—to have such a refined and dedicated young priest in their parish. Ava's family was proud. To them, Father Mark's presence in Ava's life was a gift. **Protection. Favor. Grace.**

Adam knew of him, of course. Every Sunday call, Ava spoke freely about her work with the church and how helpful Father Mark had been. She sent Adam pictures of the altar arrangements, the banners she had helped hang, the new rosaries she had picked out for the communicants. Adam would laugh gently, his voice sometimes distant, but grateful.

"It's good you have support, Ava. A priest with you, there's comfort in that. God bless him."

He didn't know—**couldn't** know—that Father Mark often lingered longer than necessary when touching her shoulder. That sometimes, his glances were too heavy, too direct. That Ava felt heat rise in her chest at the smell of his aftershave, or that when she reached out once to adjust the stray edge of his collar, her fingers tingled after.

She buried all of it deep. She had made a vow. **Five years. That was the plan. Just five.**

The morning of Margaret's First Communion was cloudless. The sun seemed to pour molten gold through the stained-glass windows, drenching the church in a glow so brilliant it felt heavenly. The pews were full—mothers in cream lace and powder-blue skirts, fathers in pressed suits, children adorned like miniature saints in white veils and small ties.

Margaret was radiant. Her white dress shimmered like spun sugar, her veil delicately pinned in place with tiny pearl clips. Her eyes searched the congregation for someone who wasn't there.

"Mommy," she whispered as they lined up before the procession. "Will Papa come later?"

Ava knelt beside her and took her daughter's face in her hands, barely holding back tears.

"Papa is praying for you right now, my love. He wishes more than anything to be here. He is with you… in your heart."

Daniel stood nearby in his suit, quiet and reserved. He didn't ask about his father anymore—but Ava saw the flicker of disappointment each time another child was embraced by their proud dad after Communion.

Inside the church, the ceremony unfolded with sacred reverence. The air smelled of incense and lilies, and the choir sang with such tenderness that some of the older women wept openly. Father Mark led the service with theatrical grace, his voice full of gravity, his smile just wide enough to feel warm but not out of place.

Margaret approached the altar, hands folded, eyes downcast like she had been taught. When the host touched her tongue, she closed her eyes, her little face serene.

Ava wept quietly in the pew.

After the ceremony, there were gifts, hugs, and dozens of photos. Daniel carried his sister on his shoulders for some of the pictures, both of them laughing—**trying** to fill the void left by Adam's absence. Ava snapped photo after photo to send across the ocean: Margaret with her grandparents, with friends, with the priest.

And then came the moment that made her stomach twist—the envelopes.

As tradition dictated, each parent handed Father Mark a small token of appreciation. Ava's envelope, once again, held five hundred dollars—her and Adam's offering of gratitude, meant to bless the man who had guided their child in faith.

Father Mark smiled—gracious, humble.

"Thank you, Ava. And thank Adam for me, too. This is very generous. Your family has such spirit."

"It's for the church," she replied softly, eyes lowering. "And for everything you've done."

He nodded. "God sees all, Ava. Especially sacrifices like yours."

That night, as she lay in bed beside Margaret—her daughter clutching her Communion prayer book under the blankets—Ava stared at the ceiling, heart aching.

Would Adam ever forgive her if he knew how much she needed comfort?

Would she ever forgive herself for needing it?

And in a quiet apartment across town, Father Mark sat alone at his desk, the envelope beside a glass of wine. He didn't open it right away. He just stared out the window, the city lights flickering in his eyes.

"They trust me," he murmured. "That's worth everything."

FOUNDATION'S BLESSING

*The long-awaited home nears completion,
symbolizing faith and stability.*

Ava sat alone on the small concrete step behind the house she and Adam had once called home. The house, though old and creaking at the joints, held memories in every nail and beam—echoes of children's laughter, whispered promises, and the scent of warm bread on Sunday mornings. But now it felt more like a museum—curated and functional, but hollow without the sound of Adam's voice filling its rooms.

She wrapped her arms tightly around her knees and leaned forward, her forehead resting on them, the sun low and cold behind drifting clouds. For a long moment, she allowed herself the truth—she didn't know who she was anymore. Not really. She was still a daughter, still a mother, a friend, a teacher… but **was she still a wife**? Or had she become some spiritual halfway thing—a sort of **quasi-widow** whose husband lived oceans away, visible only through a flickering computer screen and Sunday phone calls?

There were days when the loneliness became a tide that nearly swept her under. She'd smile for the children, make small talk for Mamma and Papa, and tend the garden and chores like clockwork—but inside, she was bone-weary. The colors of life seemed faded. Ava could no longer tell if what she felt was just sadness or the first creeping root of **bitterness**.

She had once believed—fervently—that this five-year separation would be worth it. But now, with Adam's return drawing near, she was afraid. **Did she still love him the way she once had? Would he still love her?** Or had time and silence unraveled the delicate thread of their intimacy? Sometimes, she would stare at his photos and feel a strange detachment, as if she were remembering a dream from childhood.

Papa had started to speak more openly now about his own regret—how maybe they had been wrong to encourage Adam to leave. The sorrow in Ava's eyes weighed on him, and the children—sweet Daniel and gentle Margaret—still asked with innocent confusion: *Why did Papa have to go?*

Even Mamma, once a pillar of unflinching optimism, carried quiet pain in her eyes. She watched Ava closely now, worried about how much of herself her daughter had buried.

Ava sobbed quietly, shoulders trembling, letting the emotion break free just for a moment. Her hands, still smelling faintly of garlic from preparing dinner, clutched her skirt. "How much longer, Lord?" she whispered. "How long do I carry this ache?"

And then—voices. Little feet running up the walk.

"Mommy! Mommy! We're home!"

She wiped her face quickly and forced a smile as Daniel and Margaret rushed into her arms. The burden returned to its hidden place in her soul.

They still prayed the rosary every evening together—Daniel led the decades now with the solemnity of a little monk. But

Ava rarely made it to midweek Mass. She often wondered, with deep shame, if **God had abandoned her**, too. Why else would the pain be so unrelenting?

Still, she clung to duty—cleaning, parenting, teaching, and caring for Mamma and Papa. Each night, she spent a quiet hour rubbing liniment into Papa's aching legs, the warmth of her hands easing the tightness in his calves. He never asked; she just did it. It was the only time of day when she felt at peace—silent, necessary, present.

When the foundation of their new home was finally poured, Ava called Father Mark to ask if he would accompany her to bless it.

The day they went was heavy with grey clouds, but the smell of wet earth and fresh blossoms gave the air a sense of resurrection. Rain from the night before had filled the stream that curved behind the land, and it danced over stones and fallen branches, lively and unbothered.

Father Mark stood with her at the edge of the concrete slab, reading a short blessing and making the sign of the cross with holy water. The wind rustled through the tall grass around them, and Ava closed her eyes for a moment, letting herself believe—just for a breath—that everything would be okay.

After the blessing, they walked slowly toward the woods and the stream, the sound of water lapping at the banks beside them.

"You've chosen a beautiful piece of land," he said softly, watching the current. "The children will be wild with joy in these woods. I used to play in places like this as a boy."

Ava turned to him, surprised. "Oh? I always assumed you were from the city."

He smiled faintly, but his eyes stayed fixed on the stream. "No. A small village. We had no running water... no indoor plumbing. But we had joy. My brothers and I would spend all day outside. We were free."

There was a pause, and then—quieter—he added, "One of my brothers… the youngest. He died from pneumonia. Just a baby."

Ava felt her breath catch. "I'm so sorry."

He didn't reply. Instead, he started walking back toward the car in silence.

She followed, the squelch of wet earth underfoot the only sound between them. When they reached the vehicle, Ava handed him a white envelope.

"Just a small offering," she said, quietly. "For your time… and for your blessing."

He accepted it with a nod, fingers brushing hers more intentionally than they needed to. His lips parted as if to say more, but he thought better of it.

"Thank you, Ava. May God bless this house. And your family."

They drove away, the silence between them thick—not cold, but not innocent either.

ANOTHER FIVE YEARS

*Time passes with silent longing,
endurance, and distant love.*

Joseph had become Ava's lifeline when it came to the construction of the new house. A quiet and dependable presence, he guided her through each phase of the process with the steady hand of someone who had done this before—many times. He never let her stray too far from the essentials.

"No unnecessary gadgets, Ava," he would say with a small smile and a firm tone, shaking his head at a fancy light fixture or decorative column she had impulsively picked out.

And he was always right.

Building a home in Europe was no easy feat. Progress was slow, often maddeningly so. Materials like brick were in high demand, and delays were common. While Adam had sent over shipments of tools, fixtures, and appliances that were hard to come by locally, bricks—those foundational necessities—had to be sourced with care, and Joseph helped secure every last one.

It gave Ava a sense of momentum, of purpose, something to keep her tethered when everything else felt adrift.

But that sense of momentum came to a crashing halt one rainy Thursday afternoon when Adam called.

At first, his voice was bright, almost manic with energy. He talked fast, stumbling over words, the cadence not unlike someone trying to sell a dream.

"Ava, listen to me, I've been thinking... maybe I should stay another five years. Just five more. Things are going so well now. I'm making two thousand dollars a week. Sometimes more. With overtime, we could finish the house, furnish it, travel— anywhere. The kids could see Paris, Rome, the Swiss Alps. We'd finally live like kings, Ava. Like kings."

Ava's hands froze where they were folding Daniel's clean laundry. She stood in stunned silence, the weight of his words pressing down on her chest like iron.

"Absolutely not," she said, her voice trembling, barely restrained. "It's enough. It has to be enough. You must come home. The computer screen with your smiling face is not a substitute for a husband, for a father. We need you—**I** need you. I need to kiss you, to feel your arms around me. I need to stop living this half-life. It's been five years, Adam. **Five years.**"

But Adam wouldn't let up. He was relentless, grasping at numbers, logic, potential futures. She could hear the desperation underneath his ambition—not just to provide, but to justify the enormous price they were all paying for his success.

And then came something new. Something terrifying.

She stopped fighting.

Not because he had convinced her. Not because she understood. But because deep down, a part of her had stopped caring.

She didn't scream or sob. She didn't plead anymore. Instead, her voice went quiet. Emotionless. Detached.

"Do what you must, Adam. I won't fight you."

She ended the call before he could say more, her hands shaking as she pressed the phone to her chest. The silence in the room rang louder than any scream.

Later that night, after the children were asleep, Ava sat alone in the living room under the soft hum of the lamp. Her eyes fell on the photographs on the mantle—Daniel's beaming soccer portrait, Margaret at the church altar in her First Communion dress, and between them, a smiling Adam holding both children in his arms, taken before he left.

Now Daniel was ten and obsessed with soccer. His days were filled with practices, goals, muddy uniforms, and shouts of victory. He no longer asked when Papa would come home.

Margaret had grown into a bright, gentle soul. She sang like a nightingale and played the piano with an emotional maturity far beyond her years. When she sang Ave Maria, the whole church fell silent.

They were thriving—without him.

That realization came with a wave of guilt so intense Ava thought she might collapse under it. But it was true. The children had adapted to life without their father. It was she who remained tethered to the ache.

Was this what Adam wanted? Was the house worth it if it became a monument to separation?

Her heart no longer felt the rush when she heard his voice. Their Sunday calls had become strained, formal—like pen pals exchanging updates, not lovers separated by oceans and sacrifice.

And yet… she endured. Because what else was there to do?

On Sunday, she returned from Mass with a strange sense of numbness. Margaret was rehearsing a new song in the background, and Daniel came in from soccer, laughing, grass stains on his knees. The noise of their lives filled the home, and Ava moved among them like a ghost.

She had buried her longing in construction plans and committee work. She had buried her anger in silence. And now, with Adam's decision to stay, she felt herself burying her **hope.**

But she still had her children. She still had Mamma and Papa. She still had the house, now rising slowly from the earth like a promise carved in stone.

She looked out the window toward the half-built structure in the distance.

"We'll live here," she whispered, "with or without him."

SOCIAL LIFE

*The effects of community gossip
and shifting relationships.*

For years, Adam had lived like a monk in the bustling city of Chicago. His world revolved around work, sleep, prayer, and weekly calls to his family. He'd given up everything but necessity—no vacations, no drinking, no unnecessary spending. His only indulgence was standing beside the endless shimmer of Lake Michigan, watching the waves breathe in and out, as if they too bore the weight of separation and longing.

But after his last call with Ava—after her voice trembled with rage and heartbreak, after she snapped the laptop shut and left him staring at a black screen—something inside him shifted.

Why not? he thought bitterly. *Why keep living like this—like a ghost?*

In a rare act of rebellion against his own routine, Adam decided to accept an invitation to a co-worker's wedding. He bought a new dark blue suit and polished loafers. He took his time choosing an embossed white shirt and a paisley tie threaded with rose and navy. As he gazed at himself in the mirror, he barely recognized the man staring back: broad-shouldered, clean-cut, eyes still blue as glacier ice, framed by thick blond hair. He looked good.

"This is who I was," he whispered. "This is who I could still be."

The wedding was a sensory celebration: flowers, flickering lights, joyous music. It wasn't the solemnity of church—it was alive, celebratory, and Adam found himself swaying, smiling, and then... noticing **her**.

Mary.

Blonde, blue-eyed, and petite, Mary had a quiet poise that drew him in instantly. She laughed like she meant it. When he hesitated, preparing to walk away from what he knew would be dangerous ground, she called out to him. Her voice carried a kindness that pierced through his hesitation, and soon, he was seated beside her.

"I saw you standing there. You looked like someone waiting for permission to breathe," she said softly.

They talked for hours that night. Mary was straightforward, opinionated, and disarmingly honest. She, too, was married with children—working in America to support her family back home. Their circumstances mirrored each other, and that commonality made their growing friendship feel safe. Or at least excusable.

Over the next few weeks, they saw each other more often. They met for coffee, for lunch, for occasional dinners when schedules allowed. She worked with a group of lawyers, did paralegal work, and dabbled in IT.

One evening, seated under soft lights in a quiet café, their conversation turned toward faith.

"I believe in God," Mary said, "but I don't practice. Church just... doesn't do it for me. I go a couple times a year. That's enough."

Adam blinked, baffled.

"But if you believe... how can you not go to Mass? How can you not receive the Eucharist?"

"Simple," she shrugged. "Because faith isn't confined to rituals. I live decently. I don't lie. I don't cheat. I work hard for my family. I don't need incense and Latin to be a good person."

"Faith must be expressed," Adam replied, his voice low but earnest. "The sacraments... they help us fight our weaknesses. They're not just tradition—they're strength."

Mary tilted her head, unfazed.

"My grandmother went to Mass every day. Confession weekly. Took Communion like it was medicine. And she was the most cruel, judgmental woman I've ever known. Devout? Maybe. Loving? Not even close."

Adam was quiet for a moment, absorbing that. Then he countered,

"Maybe... maybe she would've been worse without her faith."

Mary laughed softly, then grew serious.

"Adam, I knew another woman. My neighbor. She never flaunted religion, never even talked about God much. But she was generous. She was kind to everyone. She *lived* her beliefs—not for display, but as instinct."

Adam nodded slowly, then asked:

"But isn't it contradictory—to believe and not practice?"

Mary leaned forward.

"Then here's a question for you: is it possible to **practice** but not **believe**?"

Adam frowned.

"That's... not possible. Who would do that?"

Mary locked eyes with him.

"Priests."

The word hit him like a slap.

"No," he said quickly. "You're wrong. Most priests are sincere."

"Some are," she admitted. "But too many... are just performers in robes. You know it. They sell sacraments. Weddings, baptisms, funerals—prices are set. My neighbor had to sell her late wife's jewelry to afford a church burial. The priest turned them away at first because the 'donation' wasn't enough."

"That's an isolated case—"

"No, Adam. Look at the news. Read the papers. Abuse scandals. Priests who father children. Drunks in confessionals. How many are truly spiritual? And how many are just empty suits, obsessed with money and status? A priest who prays for money—what do you call that?"

Adam was silent. His thoughts spun. She wasn't wrong. He had read those headlines. He had seen the hypocrisy— sometimes even within his own parish.

"Materialism is a form of atheism," Mary said softly. "Isn't it?"

He could only nod.

"So what about you, Adam? Staying here, chasing more money, sacrificing time with your wife and children—for a house? For luxury? Is that not materialism?"

Her words sliced through him.

Was he... an atheist in disguise? Had he let greed wear the mask of sacrifice? Had he betrayed the very faith he claimed to cherish?

"I love my wife," he murmured, but it sounded hollow. "I just want to give her everything."

"Maybe she doesn't want everything," Mary said gently. "Maybe she just wants *you*."

Adam didn't answer. Because somewhere, buried beneath the guilt, confusion, and ambition, he had started to **want Mary instead**.

And he hated himself for it.

ROSARY GARDEN

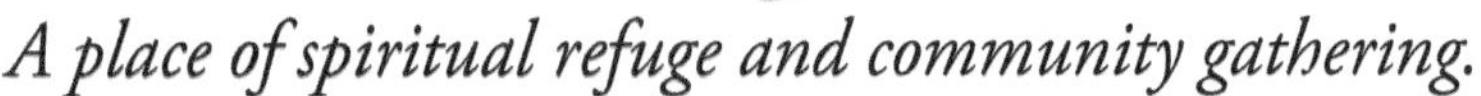

A place of spiritual refuge and community gathering.

Father John had been assigned to assist at St. Isidore's Parish—a prosperous and devout community nestled in a well-manicured suburb—after Father Felix's liver cancer progressed with alarming speed. Though physically frail, Father Felix remained spiritually resolute, his once-powerful voice now a soft echo of its former self. The parishioners adored him, not just for his decades of gentle leadership, but for the living testament of beauty and prayer he had left behind: the Rosary Garden.

It was unlike anything anyone had seen before—a sacred Eden carved into two acres of consecrated land, a place where nature and scripture danced in harmony. Father Felix had envisioned it during a pilgrimage to Lourdes, and over twenty years, piece by piece, plant by plant, it became his life's offering to the Blessed Virgin.

The garden was enclosed by a seven-foot stone wall, a barrier to the world beyond and a threshold into mystery. Cascading over its weathered surface were trumpet vines, their orange and crimson blooms like bursts of joy calling the faithful to prayer. Climbing roses—red like the blood of martyrs, white like the Immaculate Conception, pink like the joy of salvation—twined in designated sections, growing upward as if reaching for heaven itself. Purple clematis, bold and regal, wove between them, offering quiet moments of majesty, while pampas grass—feathery, pale pink and white—swayed at the garden's base like whispered Ave Marias in the wind.

The entrance was almost hidden, a wrought iron gate nearly swallowed by ivy, its curved frame giving the illusion of a secret passage to another world. Once inside, the senses were instantly engulfed—by scent, color, sound, and spirit.

The garden unfolded in three concentric circles, symbolic of the Joyful, Sorrowful, and Glorious Mysteries. Each ring was both architectural and spiritual, carefully curated to align with the prayers of the Rosary.

In the first circle, visitors encountered an alcove carved into a stone archway. A delicate fountain flowed beneath an intricately sculpted tableau of the Annunciation, Mary frozen in marble wonder as Gabriel knelt before her. Around the pool bloomed red corn poppies, radiant against their green backdrop. A single white marble bench faced the scene, inviting pilgrims to sit and meditate.

The next alcove glowed with Siberian irises, deep violet petals mirrored in a small pond alive with darting fish. Another corner featured stalks of golden wheat, planted among carpets of honey-scented alyssum, their fragrance mingling with the cool breeze. Here, cat tails rose solemnly from a still water basin—reminders of simplicity, abundance, and the sacredness of the harvest.

With each Mystery, the flowers changed. Purple larkspur and Pontic azaleas flourished around the fifth Sorrowful Mystery, a reminder of Gethsemane and the agony of sacrifice. Crocuses, hyacinths, jonquils, and tulips—the heralds of spring—surrounded the Resurrection alcove, bursting with color and symbolism of new life.

The three circles were hedged in perfection: the first lined with deep green velvet boxwood, manicured to six feet high and trimmed weekly, forming a solemn, almost monastic boundary. The second, edged with golden privet, shimmered under sunlight like halos made of leaves.

And then—at the center—stood the heart of it all: a towering marble sculpture of the Risen Christ, arms outstretched, standing in a fountain of cascading water. When the sun hit it just right, rainbows shimmered across the spray, arching in ethereal arcs that made the children gasp and adults fall to their knees. Some called it the miracle of the garden.

"The Risen Christ does not weep," Father Felix once whispered. "He welcomes. He radiates. He reminds us that the tomb is never the end."

The walkways, constructed with patient care, were laid first in garden paper and gravel and then topped with mosaic marble tiles. Shades of cream, cobalt blue, soft pink, caramel, and white danced together underfoot, woven like a heavenly tapestry. To walk them was to trace a sacred path—each step a Hail Mary, each turn an invitation to deeper reflection.

The Rosary Garden wasn't merely beautiful—it was transformative. It had become a place where people came to grieve, to hope, to propose, to seek forgiveness, to lay down burdens they had carried far too long. It was a living prayer, breathing through petals and stone.

Father John, though younger and less experienced, was deeply moved as he stepped through the garden each morning. He'd never known such peace. And he silently vowed—when the time came—to care for this garden as lovingly as Father Felix had.

Because beauty, like faith, must be tended—or it fades.

FATHER JOHN

The priest whose charisma masks deeper issues.

Father John quickly became a beloved presence in the parish. He made people feel seen and accepted, never judging, always listening. His laughter had a warmth that gathered people to him like moths to a gentle flame. Though he was small in stature, with an awkward gait and feet so unusually large that his shoes had to be ordered from special catalogs, none of that mattered to the parishioners. His humility and humor made him approachable, and his eccentricities only endeared him more to those around him.

Father Felix, weakened by his advancing illness, had asked Father John to assist with confessions. It was a heavy task in a parish where the sacrament was taken seriously and the line of penitents rarely dwindled. Father John, for reasons he kept private, often peeked through a small chink in the curtain—not to judge, but to see the human face behind the sin. For him, sin was not abstract. It was intimately tied to the lives of the broken, the desperate, the lonely. He wanted to understand it all.

One day, a young woman entered the confessional. She was elegant and composed, yet carried with her an air of sadness. She confessed to being unfaithful to her husband—a man she loved—but her desires had become overwhelming. She begged for forgiveness, struggling to understand herself, desperate to change. Her voice trembled with shame and longing, and as she wept, Father John listened quietly.

He gave her absolution, and for her penance, he instructed her to go to the Rosary Garden and pray for her family—for the strength to resist what pulled her away from them.

Later that day, Father John strolled through the garden himself. The air was thick with the fragrance of blooming lilies and roses. He wandered from one alcove to another, his rosary in hand, though his mind was elsewhere. He found her sitting alone near the Assumption alcove, surrounded by white star lilies. Their eyes met.

"Good afternoon," he said gently. "Isn't this garden a peaceful place to reflect?"

"Yes," she said, looking up with a soft smile. "It's perfect for thinking... and praying."

They exchanged a few more words—light conversation about work, the parish, and the beauty of the garden. She mentioned needing to run errands, lamenting how much she could carry on the bus.

"I have a van," he offered without hesitation. "I could help you with your shopping. If you don't mind the company."

At first, she hesitated. But his kindness felt genuine, and there was something about his presence—disarming and gentle. She accepted.

As they drove through the village, their conversation deepened. She spoke of her struggle to reconcile her faith with her desires. He listened carefully, his responses thoughtful but cautious. The line between spiritual guidance and personal interest blurred. By the time they pulled off the road near a quiet, wooded area, they were no longer priest and penitent, but two flawed people suspended in a moment of temptation.

As they drove along in Father John's dark brown van, the woman asked him why he needed such a vehicle and he told her he was a Good Samaritan. If he saw someone that needed a ride, he picked them up and drove them wherever they needed to go. Generally, they were mostly the elderly. He reached over and caressed her breast and tweaked her nipple. "Oh Father you don't waste this on the old people, do you? It feels very good." She reached over and touched his maleness and manipulated his zipper open. "Well, that feels better than I have ever felt." He suddenly swerved the van off the side of the road.

"I guess that does feel good." She said laughing. "I know of a place where we can continue this exploration. Do you have time?" "I always have time for this." She said as he slid his hand into her panties. She moaned and said: "Please hurry. Please… oohhh!"

He parked his van in a densely forested area and took her in the back of the van that was equipped with a mattress dressed in silk sheets. They tore at their clothes and she was already achieving an orgasm when he entered her. They repeated this, a multitude of times and in as many positions that their hunger drove them to.

CONFIRMATION

*The children take another step in faith
amid growing personal tensions.*

The morning of Confirmation dawned bright and full of promise. The church bells rang out across the village, echoing through the hills like a sacred announcement. It was a day of great joy and solemnity—Daniel and Margaret, along with their classmates, would receive the Sacrament of Confirmation, affirming the faith planted at their baptisms and stepping into a new spiritual maturity.

Inside the church, every pew was filled. Mothers straightened veils and smoothed collars, fathers stood silently with pride swelling in their chests. The children, dressed in their finest white robes, looked radiant and a little nervous. Margaret clutched her rosary tightly, and Daniel—now growing into the frame of a young man—stood tall beside her, his eyes scanning the sanctuary for his mother.

Ava sat with Mamma and Papa in the front pew, her heart pounding with emotion. The absence of Adam pressed against her chest like a stone, but today, she resolved, would be about her children. She smiled warmly as they processed in, each step a testament to the faith she had tried so hard to nurture in their lives.

The Bishop, a stately man with a gentle presence, took his place at the pulpit and delivered his homily. His voice resonated through the marble arches of the church with calm authority:

"When you were baptized, you were brought to the Church as children. Your parents, godparents, and priests began the work of guiding your hearts toward God. But today, you stand before us not as children, but as young adults. From this day forward, the responsibility of your faith is yours to carry. Nurture it. Defend it. Build upon it—not only for yourselves but for the generations that will come after you. Support your priests. Stand with your Church. Offer your prayers, your time, your labor—and yes, even your treasure—for the work of God on earth continues only through you."

A hushed reverence fell over the congregation. Margaret's eyes glistened with tears; Daniel stood with his chin slightly raised, absorbing the Bishop's words with youthful gravity. The sacrament was conferred with holy chrism, each candidate sealed with the gifts of the Holy Spirit—wisdom, understanding, counsel, fortitude, knowledge, piety, and fear of the Lord.

When the Mass ended, the children beamed as they walked down the aisle, confirmed in faith and glowing with hope. Friends and family gathered outside beneath the sunlight, exchanging hugs and taking photos. Daniel and Margaret ran to the Bishop to thank him, followed closely by their classmates. The Bishop placed his hands gently on each of their shoulders, offering a final blessing.

Father Thomas stood nearby, dignified and content, proud of the children and of the parish he had shepherded.

He and the Bishop would soon leave together for a brief retreat in the mountains—a custom of rest and reflection after a sacramental season.

Meanwhile, Father Mark stood surrounded by well-wishers and parents. As always, he accepted praise with his signature polished smile. An envelope was handed to him by the confirmation committee—another generous token of appreciation from the parish. He accepted it gracefully, knowing from experience that it likely held cash.

Later, as he returned to his quarters, he would find a separate envelope from Ava. As expected, inside was five hundred dollars—perhaps more. After all, both of her children had been prepared under his spiritual leadership. He had guided their confessions, instructed them on the mysteries of the Church, and overseen their rehearsals. The envelope confirmed what he already suspected: Ava's gratitude, her trust, and her financial generosity were still intact.

He placed the envelope inside his briefcase, his expression unreadable. The congregation had their celebration. He had his reward.

LIVING TOGETHER

*Adam begins a secret life with
another woman in the U.S.*

Whenever Adam had a rare free moment, he called
Mary. At first, their conversations were casual—
lighthearted chats about life in America, stories
about their homelands, and shared frustrations about long hours
and cold winters. But over time, their talks deepened. Adam
spoke fondly of his village, its winding streets, its slow growth,
the laughter of children at dusk. Mary spoke with a mixture of
pride and sorrow about her husband and children back home,
about the crowded city where they lived, and how little her
husband earned working long shifts in a glass factory.

When the opportunity came for her to work abroad, she
hadn't hesitated. Her education opened doors. She didn't see it
as abandoning her family but as providing for them in a way
she never could at home.

Their bond grew quietly—first through laughter, then
through confessions of deeply personal things: their likes,

dislikes, fears. They never spoke of their spouses. That was the line they would not cross. Or so they told themselves. Their marriages became the invisible boundary neither dared analyze aloud. It was safer that way.

Mary, ever practical, helped Adam save money—introducing him to coupons, rebates, and savvy grocery shopping tricks. She calculated everything down to the penny, and the extra cash allowed them to enjoy occasional dinners out or a movie on Friday nights. They became inseparable companions. So when Mary one day suggested they move in together—strictly for convenience, she said—it felt like a natural progression. Just two friends helping each other.

Adam hesitated.

The thought of living with another woman—while still married to Ava—gnawed at his conscience. His faith raised alarms, as did the thought of gossip. What if someone found out and word reached his family? Still, the situation seemed increasingly reasonable, especially after Mary confided that her current living conditions were unbearable. Her roommate's drinking, late-night parties, and string of boyfriends had turned the apartment into a place of chaos.

In contrast, Adam craved peace.

Eventually, logic won over guilt.

They found a modest apartment in a quiet part of town, far enough from co-workers to avoid suspicion. Adam was delighted that the place was still within walking distance of the lake—his sacred refuge. The apartment had two bedrooms, a spacious kitchen, a cozy living room, and a bathroom situated between their sleeping quarters. Everything was stark white when they moved in, but after a trip to the thrift store, they transformed the space with secondhand drapes and a palette of soft blues. Even the mismatched sofa and lamps somehow matched. A used television was the final touch. They laughed together as they arranged the furniture, a sense of domestic harmony slowly creeping in.

Then one evening, as the wind howled outside and snow coated the windows, everything changed.

They were watching a movie together—shoulders touching, warmth exchanged in subtle gestures. Adam draped his arm around her. She leaned in without hesitation. It had been years since he felt the softness of a woman beside him, the intimacy of unspoken affection. His breath caught when her fingers intertwined with his. Their kiss began gently, tentatively— then deepened. She clung to him as if she'd been starving for this kind of closeness. He held her tightly and whispered into her hair:

"Oh, Mary… I understand. I feel the same way."

What followed was inevitable. Adam carried her to his bed. Slowly, reverently, he touched every part of her, as if memorizing a language he had long forgotten. Mary trembled under his hands, her eyes searching his for permission, forgiveness, something sacred. When their bodies joined, their release was simultaneous—a surrender to the longing they'd buried for too long.

Wrapped in each other's arms, breath mingling, they whispered about how much they cared for each other. And when their passion reignited, they didn't resist. The rules were forgotten. The guilt vanished, buried under the weight of desire.

In the morning, Mary woke first. She stroked his hair, then reached for him under the covers. Adam stirred and murmured Ava's name in a half-conscious haze. Mary froze. Her hand withdrew.

"My name is Mary, you slug," she said, laughing—but with a sharpness that stung.

Adam sat up, dazed. "I'm sorry, Mary. I was dreaming… Come here. Let me make it up to you."

"It's okay," she said softly, curling into him. "I know we'll go back to our families one day. But right now… I'm here. We're here."

He kissed her gently, thankful she understood what even he could not fully explain.

God forgive him—but he loved her. Not in the deep, covenantal way he loved Ava, no. But Mary had become part of him. They shared a life now, a rhythm. They cooked together, laughed, made love, and watched the seasons change from their apartment windows. It was a fragile happiness, but it was real.

The weekends brought tension. He still called home, though the calls grew shorter. Sometimes he forgot altogether. When Ava asked why, he blamed long hours or technical issues. The truth—that he had spent the weekend in bed with another woman—was a truth he refused to admit even to himself.

But the end of his contract loomed. Soon, he would have to return. And when he did, what would he be returning to? Who?

He reminded himself: *Ava. Daniel. Margaret.*

That was his life. His *real* life.

But why did it feel so far away?

HOUSE'S BLESSING

Ava's dream home is finally completed and blessed.

It was August, and the linden trees had exploded into bloom. Their sweet, heady fragrance clung to the warm air and drew bees in droves. Ava stood beneath one of the oldest trees in her garden, reaching gently into the branches, competing with the honeybees for the delicate golden blossoms. Her woven basket was nearly full—the blooms would be dried and steeped into a calming tincture, a traditional remedy for winter colds and seasonal grief.

As her fingers plucked the last few flowers, a familiar voice called out.

"Hello, my neighbor! Are you preparing medicine for my winter aches and pains?"

It was Joseph, his smile warm, his tone light, though his eyes searched her face more deeply than the words suggested.

Ava smiled, though there was sorrow behind it. "Yes, Joseph. The village might be in great need of it. Hopefully, the flu won't come around this year." Her voice trembled slightly, a gentle crack betraying the loneliness that lived behind her steady expression.

He caught it, but let it pass with grace. "Looks like you've harvested enough to cure an entire town. Save some blossoms for the bees, Ava!" he teased, waving as he headed toward his car.

He was short on time. Father Felix's condition had worsened, and Joseph had another "collector" to finish—a commissioned cabinet of carved wood for the rectory. The old priest's liver cancer was progressing fast. Time, now, felt as precious as breath—measured, sacred, slipping.

Before he drove off, Ava called out, "We're moving into the new house this week. Can you come help?"

"I'll be there," he replied, without hesitation.

"I knew I could rely on you," she said softly, almost to herself.

The new house—her dream and burden—was ready, or as ready as it could be. She had chosen a soft dove-gray carpet for the family room, the very heart of the home. A fireplace stood proudly at the center wall, awaiting firewood and laughter. The entertainment center was on its way, and furniture would come gradually—after she studied the way light entered the rooms at different times of day, how shadows danced at dusk, how the summer breeze smelled through each open window.

For now, only the essentials would be moved in: makeshift beds, a table, and kitchen utensils. The rest could wait.

Adam's parents had decided to remain in the small, aging house they had lived in all their lives. Their pride in Adam and Ava was evident in every story they told, every photo on their mantel. Adam—so brave, leaving for America to build them a better future. Ava—so strong, raising Daniel and Margaret, caring for her in-laws as tenderly as if they were her own.

Papa was now retired, his health failing. Mamma's knees ached and her breath was shorter these days. But their hearts remained firmly rooted in their home. *This* was their world.

It had been nearly ten years since Adam left. Though the computer helped—Joseph had set it up years ago, and Ava still marveled at seeing Adam's face across oceans—nothing could replace his physical presence. Sometimes the screen only made his absence more palpable. She could see him, but not hold him. She could hear his voice, but not smell his skin or feel the weight of his arms around her.

That evening, Ava walked alone to the new house. She began organizing the kitchen, preparing drawers for the dozens of humble tools and items that formed the soul of a household. As she lined the silverware tray, she began to speak aloud, softly, like a chant.

"Adam… Adam… Adam…"

She said his name again and again, as if the repetition might somehow conjure him, might tear open the veil of distance and bring him to her side. She was stunned when the tears came— she hadn't expected them. She thought they had dried up long ago. But they returned, heavy and uninvited, and spilled down her cheeks as if the house itself demanded a baptism of sorrow and love.

A few days later, the family gathered. Father Mark came in his clerical blacks, his warm presence grounding everyone. Ava stood beside him, her children on either side, as he raised his hand and blessed the home. The sun shimmered through the clean windows as the words of consecration flowed from his lips.

"May this home be a sanctuary. A place of peace, of laughter, of shelter. May all who enter find rest and love within its walls."

Four years it had taken. Four long, steady years. And Joseph had been there for every step—helping Ava interpret architectural plans, overseeing contractors, managing imported supplies Adam had sent from America. With his connections, inspections were smooth, construction uninterrupted. And he had asked for nothing in return. Helping Ava, Joseph once said, was the only payment he needed. And she believed him.

When the ceremony was done, Ava handed Father Mark an envelope with deep thanks. He accepted it gently, then held her hand longer than expected, his fingers lacing briefly with hers.

She didn't pull away.

"Come," he said. "Let me show you something."

He led her behind the house, where a sleek, elegant vehicle waited in the gravel driveway.

"This is your new car?" she gasped. "A Mercedes! Father, it's beautiful—deep blue. It suits you. You deserve it. You work so hard, and our parish is thriving."

She gave him a warm, spontaneous hug—then pulled back quickly, scanning to see if anyone had noticed. But the moment was theirs alone.

Then she called out, her voice light again:

"Come see, everyone! Come around back—Father's new car!"

Her family appeared from around the front of the house, their faces lighting up as they admired the gleaming vehicle. The children ran their hands along the polished doors; Mamma and Papa nodded approvingly. And in that moment—brief but whole—Ava felt the stirrings of something new.

A beginning.

A home.

A hope.

FATHER THOMAS

*An unexpected revelation of corruption
and forbidden desire.*

The Bishop and Father Thomas were sitting naked in bed talking, after having an incredible sexual encounter. They applauded themselves for their virility and both enjoyed an expensive Cuban cigar. They were in the Bishop family house master bedroom, the room he was born in, as a matter of fact actually in this very bed. Tom suggested a bath and the Bishop agreed.

They fondled each other as the large tub filled with steaming water and aromatic bath salts. They kissed deeply several times and then stepped into the tub and knelt down. Tom turned his back to the Bishop and put his hands on the rim of the tub so he presented the place he and the Bishop sought for their ultimate pleasure.

Afterwards the Bishop said: "Now we must consider the appointment, whom shall we appoint as successor to Father Felix after his death?"

The Bishop said getting up from the bed and pouring them each a snifter of cognac. "I thought you, would be my number one choice." The Bishop said. "No, no! Not me! I don't care about money or prestige and I'm happy right where I am. You know I don't like to visit the hospital and talk to the patient every day. It will make me upset and sick. Another thing: a lot of confessions. I do not want to spend my life in confessional box. The people, in Father Felix parish, go to confession like crazy. They confess their sins like parrots. I do not want to lose the taste of my life. By the way: when we will practice general absolution? This is the time for it."

"My Thomas, do not tell people anything about general absolution. If we do this, we surely lose the control upon people." Bishop responded clearly. "I have never considered confession as a kind of control upon the people." Father Tomas answered.

"Theologically not, but psychologically it is." "You are almost right, but in addition, this all takes time, which I prefer to spend with you, my love. Perhaps Father John could continue on as pastor. He has been an Associate for some time now.

Please my beloved choose him." Tom said. "I don't know. I am not sure. He is good Associate, but would he be a good Pastor as well? Perhaps, Father Mark would be the best. He is so exemplary, but he does not have as much experience as Father John. I think he is not ready yet. So Tom, see what you can find out about Father John. I am ready to nominate him with your intersection." "Okay, when we return at the end of our special time together, I'll check it out. You know that he is not like us, he is heterosexual." "Come hear my dear love and let me hold you closely." The Bishop said. And they reaffirmed their love for each other again.

FATHER JOHN'S CONFESSION

*A scandalous admission threatens
the integrity of the priesthood.*

Father Mark was known far and wide as a priest of unwavering integrity, a pillar of discretion, and a master of the confessional. His sermons on the sacred seal of confession were legendary. Parishioners respected him, and his brother priests often sought his guidance, drawn by his quiet authority and patient ear.

He would sit for hours, listening to penitent after penitent unburden their hearts—often the same trivial sins repeated by the same habitual confessors. He never showed weariness. But when Father John walked into his study one evening asking for confession, Father Mark immediately sensed this would be different.

Father John was, on the surface, an unlikely man to stir such intrigue. Rugged and stout, with a face better suited for the boxing ring than the pulpit, he somehow possessed a natural magnetism. Women, especially, were drawn to his warmth, his earthy laugh, and his uncanny ability to adapt to anyone in his company. With the working-class, he spoke plainly and shared in their burdens. With the educated, his vocabulary shifted effortlessly to match theirs. He made people feel seen—and that, Father Mark had always silently admitted, was a gift.

But tonight, there was no trace of Father John's usual charm. They sat in silence on the worn leather sofa in Father Mark's modest living room, the lamplight casting solemn shadows across their faces. Then, John broke the silence.

"I broke the sixth commandment," he said flatly.

Father Mark inhaled slowly. "How many times?"

"Too many to count."

Father Mark's voice remained calm, though a flicker of surprise crossed his face. "And how long has this been going on?"

"Almost a year," Father John admitted, his voice low.

"And only now you come to confess?"

"I know," John sighed. "I should've come sooner."

"Who is the woman?"

"She's married," John said, eyes fixed on the floor. "She just had her second child not long ago."

Father Mark's brows knitted together. "Is the child yours?"

"I don't know," John confessed. "Her husband believes it's his. He's devoted to her. Loyal. Loving. Blind, perhaps—but good."

A silence hung between them like incense smoke.

"Why did you do it, John? Was it love?"

"No," he said quickly. "It wasn't love. It started with opportunity—stolen moments, idle talk that became something more. She craved something her husband couldn't give her. And I… I couldn't resist."

Father Mark folded his hands and leaned back, weary. "You realize this kind of scandal never remains hidden. Someone always finds out."

"I know," John replied, almost defiantly. "But what we shared—what I felt—no bishop, no authority in the Church, can take that away from me."

Father Mark looked at him sharply. "Pleasure is fleeting. Reputation, trust, vocation—those are not. The Bishop could suspend you. You know that."

"I know," John murmured, and then, after a beat, added bitterly, "God forgives. The Church... it remembers."

"Are you sorry for your sins?" Father Mark asked quietly.

"I am," John said, his voice cracking for the first time. "I don't know how I got here. I want absolution. I need it."

Father Mark studied the man before him—not the priest in vestments, but the flawed, fractured soul seeking redemption.

"I will grant you absolution, but hear me clearly, John. Do not destroy that woman's marriage. For the sake of her children, let them believe in the goodness of their home. And for her husband—who believes in God, in the Church, in *us*—do not shatter his faith."

John nodded slowly, the weight of guilt finally evident in his downcast eyes.

"As your penance," Father Mark continued, "pray every day for the strength to master your temptation. Pray that you do not become the instrument of someone else's ruin. And pray, John... that you may still be a shepherd after all of this."

John bowed his head. "I will, Father."

And for a long moment, the only sound was the ticking of the clock in the corner—the quiet rhythm of time moving forward, carrying both sin and the hope of redemption.

CONFIDENTIAL CONVERSATION

Backroom politics determine the future of the parish.

After returning from his restful vacation with the Bishop, Father Thomas found himself seated at a quiet dinner table with Father Mark. The air was heavy with the scent of roasted lamb and unspoken agendas. Between sips of red wine and clinks of silverware, Father Thomas leaned in slightly, lowering his voice.

"You know, Father Mark," he began with measured calm, "Father Felix's time is drawing near. His condition has worsened. The Bishop is beginning to consider candidates to take over the parish."

Father Mark paused mid-bite, the fork hovering in the air. "It's one of the most affluent parishes in the diocese," Father Thomas continued. "Its donors are generous and loyal. Naturally, the Bishop wants someone… exceptional."

Mark raised a brow, curious and cautious. "And who does His Excellency have in mind?"

Father Thomas offered a subtle smile. "He's asked me about Father John."

"Father John?" Mark repeated, nearly choking on his drink. He coughed, reaching for his napkin.

"Yes. It seems the people think quite highly of him. The Bishop values that kind of support. But I wanted your take. Do you think he would make a capable pastor?"

Mark dabbed his mouth slowly, buying time. He weighed his words carefully. "Father John… He is, without question, a good priest. I've never had reason to complain. He's served for many years, he's compassionate, and yes, the people adore his sense of humor. Always cheerful, always… available." He gave a slight nod. "If the Bishop selects him, I suppose it would be a logical choice."

Father Thomas leaned back in his chair, examining Mark's response like a chess player anticipating a countermove.

"Of course, this is all strictly confidential," Thomas added. "The Bishop hasn't made anything official yet. You understand how it works… Father John would be the last to know."

"Of course," Father Mark replied quickly. "You know me, Father Thomas. This conversation never happened."

Thomas nodded approvingly, then allowed a brief pause before probing deeper.

"Now, every man has two sides… just like a coin. You've spoken well of his public face. But have you ever heard whispers about the other side? Anything—how shall I put it—less than desirable? The Bishop doesn't want to make a misstep. Especially not in a parish this visible."

A flicker crossed Mark's eyes. This was the opportunity he had been quietly praying for. He straightened, the perfect blend of piety and discretion.

"I hesitate to speak out of turn," Mark began slowly, his tone layered with false reluctance, "and I have no solid evidence. Just… murmurs. Nothing confirmed."

Thomas leaned in, voice barely above a whisper. "Tell me what you've heard."

"Well…" Mark said, lowering his voice, "there's talk of a woman. A married woman. Recently gave birth. Her husband is devoted—perhaps too trusting. It's said that Father John has spent… time with her. Alone. And we all know about his habit of driving people around in that old van of his. Always eager to help, of course." He gave a slight, meaningful smile. "But you know how tongues wag. Especially when it comes to priests."

Thomas nodded gravely. "Yes, yes, the cracks in the doors are always listening. But still… even rumors can leave a stain if not addressed properly. Thank you, Father Mark. You've done your duty to the Church."

Mark inclined his head humbly, but inside, his heart was racing. The parish would be his. All he had to do now… was wait.

NOMINATION

*Father Mark is named the new pastor,
sparking celebration and sorrow.*

Father Felix passed away quietly, just two weeks before Christmas. The village, still blanketed in early snow, was cloaked in solemnity. His devoted parishioners, stunned by the loss, gathered in the Rosary Garden despite the bitter cold. For three days and nights, they lit candles and prayed the Rosary in shifts, their voices low and unwavering, a final vigil for the priest who had given them so much.

They buried him in the church cemetery beneath the bare branches of the linden trees, their prayers lifted skyward on icy breath. Even in grief, most of the faithful assumed one thing with certainty: that Father John, his long-time associate, would naturally succeed him. With this quiet assumption, they returned to preparing for Christmas—mourning and celebration braided together in faith.

But on the first Sunday following the funeral, everything changed.

The church was packed. Candles flickered beside wreaths of evergreen and crimson ribbon. The choir had just finished the Kyrie when Father Thomas stepped up to the pulpit. His voice was steady, but his eyes carried the weight of news that would ripple through the community.

"My dear friends," he began, "as you all know, our beloved Father Felix has gone home to God. Let us continue to honor him with our prayers and good works in his memory."

A wave of bowed heads followed.

"But today," he continued, "I bring you a message of both continuity and grace. His Excellency, the Bishop, after prayerful consideration, has chosen a new shepherd for this parish."

A beat of silence passed—hearts paused, minds already filled with Father John's name.

"I am pleased to announce," Father Thomas said with a measured smile, "that Father Mark will be your new pastor."

There was a collective gasp—a sharp intake of breath that rustled the congregation like wind through trees. For a moment, confusion registered. Then came the slow ripple of applause, growing louder, eventually blooming into a full chorus of congratulations. Parishioners stood, smiling, reaching out to shake Father Mark's hand as he made his way down the aisle, gracious and humble in his acceptance.

Everyone applauded—except Ava.

Later that afternoon, Father Mark found her in the rectory's meeting room, seated on the familiar blue velvet couch they'd once shared, making plans for the children's First Communion. She looked different now. Composed, but guarded. Her fingers fidgeted with the hem of her coat.

"What is wrong with me?" she asked softly, her tone laced with a wry humor that barely masked the ache. "Why does everyone I care about leave me?"

Father Mark hesitated, caught off guard by the vulnerability behind her smile. "Who told you something is wrong with you? No one is leaving you."

She met his eyes, unflinching. "You know exactly what I'm talking about. First my husband leaves for America, and now you—off to your new parish, your new life."

He lowered himself into the chair across from her. His voice dropped. "Ava, please. I swear to you—I'll think of you often. Maybe... even more than he does."

A flicker of concern passed across his face. He feared her disappointment might turn volatile. She had the kind of spirit that could lift or sink a man's reputation with a single word.

"And now," she continued, "you'll be pastor of a wealthy parish. You'll be very busy. Too busy to remember me."

"Ava, stop," he said, a little too quickly. "I told you—I will never forget you."

She tilted her head, studying him. "But we won't see each other anymore, will we?"

He sighed and looked away. "Not for a while. I'll need time to learn the new parish. It's not just Sunday Mass—it's hospital rounds, counseling, administration... I'll be buried."

She paused, then smiled. "Relax. I was only teasing. I know who you are, Mark. And you know who I am."

Relief washed over him. "Thank God. For a moment there, I was scared."

"I know you were." Her eyes glinted with quiet mischief.

There was a pause.

"It's almost Christmas," she said, brushing a lock of hair behind her ear. "I'll need to go to confession."

Father Mark stiffened. "Not with me. And definitely not with Father Thomas," he said sharply. "That would be... catastrophic."

"Why?" Her voice trembled slightly. "Is it that bad?"

He reached for her hand. "You need someone impartial. Go to the monastery. Find Father Fabian. He's discreet, wise, and has no ties here. He's the best confessor I know."

Ava looked down, her fingers curling into her palm. "Are you sure?"

"I'm sure. Do this for yourself. For your soul."

She nodded, slowly. Then stood.

"Thank you, Mark. Merry Christmas."

And as she walked away, the scent of linden and sorrow lingered in the room.

AVA'S CONFESSION

*A moment of painful honesty
and spiritual reckoning.*

Snow fell lightly outside the stone walls of the centuries-old monastery, blanketing the garden in quiet purity. Ava stepped into the warmth of the chapel vestibule, her heart thudding beneath her winter coat. The air smelled of incense and candle wax, the sanctuary hushed except for the occasional echo of footsteps on the polished floor.

It was just days before Christmas.

Following Father Mark's careful instruction, Ava had come here—to this remote monastery—seeking more than forgiveness. She needed refuge. She needed someone who would not see her, would not judge her, and who could absorb her truth without unraveling her world.

She had avoided Father Thomas, the parish pastor. His probing questions and disapproving gaze made confession feel more like interrogation. And Father Mark—sweet, devoted Mark—was too close to the sin itself.

Which is why she had come to **Father Fabian**, a nearly blind, retired monk in his mid-eighties who had become something of a legend among penitents.

Father Fabian's only duty now was to sit for long hours in the dark wooden confessional and offer reconciliation to the wounded and weary. His blindness made him the perfect confessor for the shamed. He could not recognize faces. His memory, fleeting and inconsistent, meant sins confessed often vanished from his mind before the penitent even rose to leave. But his hearing—keen, unnervingly sharp—was unmatched. He could detect the slightest tremble in a whisper, the flutter of remorse between syllables.

Ava entered the booth slowly, her voice barely above breath. "Bless me, Father, for I have sinned."

From the other side of the screen, a raspy but gentle voice replied, "How long since your last confession, my child?"

"A few months," she answered. "I've been... waiting for the right time. The right place."

"And is today the time?"

"Yes, Father. I've committed adultery."

There was a pause, but not of shock—only quiet processing. "Are you married?"

"I am. My husband is in America. He's been away a long time. Years. I don't know how many more I can endure."

"And the adultery—it happened once?"

"No, Father. Many times."

"I see. Is this... an emotional affair? Or do you love this man?"

Ava's voice wavered. "No. I love my husband. I always have. But the distance—it's hollowed me out. There are nights I can't breathe from the loneliness. And sometimes, I fail. I fall."

"Your weakness is not unfamiliar," Father Fabian said, his tone neither condemning nor permissive. "And who is this man?"

"There are two," Ava admitted. Her voice was a mix of shame and exhaustion. "One is my neighbor, Joseph. He's married, has children. It's not about love. Just... brokenness."

There was a sharp inhalation on the other side of the screen.

"And the other?" the priest asked carefully.

She hesitated. "The other... is Father Mark. Our Associate Pastor."

A long silence followed. Then, in a voice nearly hoarse, the priest responded:

"Oh, dear Lord... A priest? My child, do you understand what this could mean—for both of you?"

"I do. But it's not as it seems. He's not a predator. We were both fragile. It happened slowly. Then all at once. But we've been careful. We've kept it hidden. No one suspects."

"Have you considered what would happen if this were exposed? To his vocation? His future? The trust of the people?"

"We've talked about it," she said, barely holding back tears. "We know the consequences. We don't intend to destroy anyone. We are... careful."

"You say that," Father Fabian said slowly, "but sin, even hidden, always leaves a trail. And what if—God forbid—you were to become pregnant?"

"We take precautions. Always. We understand the risk."

"You are not without self-awareness," the priest admitted. "But you are trapped in something dangerous. Something that doesn't belong to you."

"I know," she whispered.

There was another pause, filled only with the creaking of wood and the distant toll of a bell.

"You must begin again," he said gently. "You must return to what is yours: your marriage, your vow. Your path back may be slow, but it is there."

"I want that. I want my husband to return. I want my family back. I want peace."

"Then begin with prayer. For your penance, you will pray the Rosary—every bead offered for priests, bishops, and nuns. They carry burdens few see."

Tears streamed silently down her cheeks.

"Yes, Father."

"Go in peace. And do not let shame keep you from the light again. God sees your sorrow. Let Him lead you out of this."

Ava rose from the booth. She walked into the fading afternoon light, her breath clouding in the cold air, her body lighter than it had been in months.

And for the first time in a long time, she felt the flicker of hope.

ADAM'S CONFESSION IN THE USA

*Adam's attempt to reconcile faith
and sin ends in heartbreak.*

It had been years since Adam last stepped into a confessional. Back in his village, the rhythm of the liturgical year had always guided him—Advent, Christmas, Lent, Easter— each season a drumbeat of faith, family, and forgiveness. But in America, time moved differently. Holidays were swallowed by work. Sunday blurred into Monday. And sin, like a shadow, trailed behind him unnoticed—until now.

Christmas was coming. And for Adam, Christmas without Holy Communion felt like a table without bread. A season without light. He couldn't imagine kneeling at Midnight Mass with empty hands and a heavy heart.

So, on a snowy December morning, Adam entered a modest parish in a quiet suburb—alone, uncertain, and deeply ashamed. Adam didn't have an advisor like his wife Ava had—no priest like Father Mark to guide him, no devoted wife to gently point him toward the right confessor. That absence would ultimately cost him the very forgiveness he was so desperately seeking.

The screen slid open. A priest's voice, steady and unfamiliar, greeted him.

"Bless me, Father, for I have sinned," Adam began, his voice thick with emotion. "It has been a long time since my last confession."

"What would you like to confess, my son?"

Adam took a breath. "I've committed adultery."

"Are you married?"

"Yes."

"How many times have you committed this sin?"

Adam hesitated. "Many... too many to count. It began slowly. And then... it became my life."

The priest's tone remained even. "Why did you do this?"

"I've been separated from my wife for years. She's in my home country, raising our children while I work here. I was lonely. Weak. I met someone in a similar situation. She, too, is married, but lives apart from her husband. We found comfort in each other."

"So she is married as well?"

"Yes."

The silence that followed was long and weighty.

"Do you understand the damage this has caused?" the priest asked. "To her marriage? To your own? To your children?"

"I do," Adam said softly. "Every day, I carry the guilt. But I also carry the burden of responsibility—financially, emotionally. We've built a life here together. It wasn't supposed to happen this way, but it did."

"Do you still live with her?"

"Yes. We share an apartment. Like a married couple."

"You have families back home... and yet here, you live as though those families don't exist."

Adam's voice cracked. "I know. I live with this every day. But if I walk away now, it could devastate both of our families. We're tied together financially—rent, bills, obligations. It's not so simple."

The priest's voice was measured. "Are you ready to end this relationship?"

Adam hesitated. "Not immediately. But I've already made a plan to return home. Within a year, maybe two at most. I will be with my wife again. With my children. This is not forever. But right now... I cannot just walk away."

The silence on the other end deepened.

"My son, I believe you're sincere in your desire to make things right," the priest finally said. "But reconciliation with God cannot wait on convenience. Good intentions are not enough. Forgiveness—true absolution—requires contrition and a firm resolution to sin no more."

Adam was silent. His eyes stung with tears.

"I want to change," he whispered. "I truly do. I just... don't know how to do it all at once. I feel trapped."

"Then let this be the beginning. Not absolution, but God's blessing—for strength, for courage, for clarity. You cannot receive Communion while living in a state of ongoing sin. But grace is still possible. You must begin detaching from this false life. If your return home is truly near, start preparing your heart now."

The priest paused, then said with quiet compassion, "May God bless you and guide you on this journey. When you are ready to choose fully, come back. The door will be open."

Adam's hands trembled in his lap. The words stung, not because they were cruel—but because they were true. He had come seeking forgiveness, and instead found the sharp edge of truth. But perhaps that, too, was a form of mercy.

He left the church with his coat buttoned tightly against the cold, tears hot against his frozen cheeks. Christmas would come, and he would sit quietly in the pew. No bread, no wine— only silence. And a longing for home.

CHRISTMAS EVE MASS

Parallel lives unfold in one sacred night,
heavy with guilt and silent love.

For Ava, Christmas had always been sacred—a holy remembrance wrapped in tradition, song, candlelight, and faith. This year, however, it meant more than that. It was a redemption. A return.

She stood in line for Holy Communion, her heart fluttering with a quiet sense of victory. She had confessed, repented, and was finally at peace. The sins that once weighed her down had been surrendered in a monastery confessional to a nearly blind monk named Father Fabian—his voice like gravel, his words like balm. As she approached the altar, she looked up. Father Mark stood before her, offering the Body of Christ. Their eyes met for a brief second, and she allowed herself a small smile. A silent understanding passed between them: *It is done. I am forgiven.*

Father Mark, ever composed, returned her smile with a discreet one of his own. He was relieved. She had gone. She had chosen the right path. And now, they both could breathe a little easier.

Adam sat in a pew on the opposite side of the church, tucked among strangers, a continent away from everything he once called home. The grandeur of Christmas Eve Mass—the soaring hymns, the golden vestments, the flickering candlelight—should have filled him with warmth. Instead, he felt hollow.

As parishioners around him stood and moved toward the altar to receive Holy Communion, Adam remained seated, his body rigid, his soul aching. He couldn't go. He *shouldn't* go. He knew that now. His confession days earlier had ended in disappointment and humiliation. The priest had not absolved him. Not because he lacked remorse—but because he wasn't yet willing to change. The priest had said it clearly: *"Good intentions are not enough. You must first choose to leave the sin behind."*

Adam's hands clenched. His heart thudded. Then, in the middle of the solemn procession, he dropped to his knees and wept. Quietly, but completely. Tears spilled down his cheeks as he bowed his head, hiding his shame from the world.

What he didn't know was that Mary was there too.

She had slipped into the church just before Mass began, unnoticed, and taken a seat a few rows behind him. She saw his bowed head, his trembling shoulders. She recognized the burden on his back because she had helped carry it. And in that moment, Mary realized something deeper was happening to the man she had come to love.

Mary's relationship with the Church was complicated. Her faith was rooted in Catholicism, but shaped by reason, experience, and quiet rebellion. She remembered vividly a conversation she'd once had at a wedding rehearsal—her Catholic friend marrying a devout Lutheran. The priest had said Catholics couldn't receive Communion in a Lutheran church due to doubts over apostolic succession. The Lutheran pastor, however, had offered something radically different:

"We do not apply moral conditions to receive the Lord. We are all sinners. It is not your perfection, but your faith, that invites you to the table."

That stayed with Mary.

Since that day, she only attended Mass occasionally. She never went to confession. But she always received Communion, confident in her belief that faith alone was sufficient. In her view, it was absurd to judge who was worthy—especially when even priests, cloaked in holy vestments, carried sins of their own.

So when it was her turn, Mary walked forward and received the Host. Not out of arrogance—but out of belief. She believed Christ knew her heart. And if that wasn't enough, nothing else would be.

She returned to her pew just as Adam wiped his eyes. He hadn't seen her. But she had seen everything.

That night, back home in their shared apartment, Mary found him sitting at the edge of their bed, shoulders hunched, face distant.

"You haven't been sleeping," she said gently. "You hardly speak anymore. Are things… alright with your family?"

He shook his head. "My family is fine."

She sat beside him. "Then tell me, Adam… is it your soul that's not okay?"

Adam looked at her, startled.

"You think you're a sinner. I can see it."

He dropped his gaze, ashamed. "I am."

Mary touched his hand. "Adam, you're a good man. You're kind, honest, loyal… And yes, sensitive. You carry your guilt like a saint carries a cross."

"I just…" he struggled to form the words. "I couldn't receive Communion tonight. I felt like a fraud. I live in sin… and I know it."

Mary looked at him for a long moment, then spoke softly.

"Let me ask you something. If you slept with a different woman every night—just one-night stands—you could go to confession and be forgiven, right?"

He hesitated. "I suppose… yes."

"But because you live with me, under one roof, loving one woman consistently, you're denied absolution?"

"…Yes."

She chuckled bitterly. "So, if I were a prostitute, you'd be allowed to receive Communion."

Adam was stunned.

"Don't you see how backward that is?" she pressed. "I'm not a prostitute. I'm the woman who shares your life. Your struggles. Your secrets. And yet, you're punished for stability, not promiscuity."

He stared at her, mind reeling.

"So now, you must choose," Mary said, her voice calm but firm. "Do you want one partner who truly loves you—or a string of meaningless nights to meet the Church's loophole? What matters more—their rules, or your truth?"

Adam said nothing. But something inside him was shifting.

Mary kissed his forehead gently and stood. "I'll leave you alone to think. But Adam… you're not lost. Just deciding where home really is."

NEW PASTOR

*Father Mark embraces his new role as
pastor as Ava quietly fades into his past.*

The church bells tolled with a jubilant cadence as Father Mark stood before his new congregation for the first time as their officially appointed pastor. The scent of incense still lingered in the air, mingling with the soft murmur of prayers and greetings. Father Felix's memory hung like a gentle cloud, but now the parish was moving forward—guided by a new shepherd.

The parishioners, bundled in their winter coats, lined up after Mass to greet Father Mark in the fellowship hall. Their faces were warm, hopeful, many filled with admiration. He had long been known for his charisma, his gentle smile, and the calm authority in his voice. To many, he seemed a man both of God and of grace—handsome, articulate, and deeply spiritual.

A quiet, elderly parishioner leaned in during the receiving line and whispered with restrained excitement:

"Thank God, Father. We prayed you'd be the one. They said the Bishop was planning to assign Father John, but… well, thank God someone spoke up before it was too late. It's been said he's involved with a married woman…"

Father Mark held his smile and gently raised his hand in calm dismissal.

"Please, do not believe all you hear. Much of it is gossip, and the Church is no stranger to shadows and misunderstandings. Father John is a devoted priest. He requested to serve in the African mission fields, and the Bishop graciously honored that call."

The parishioner blinked, a little embarrassed by her own eagerness.

"Well… regardless, we're grateful to have *you*. May God bless your service among us."

"Thank you," Father Mark replied, bowing his head. "Pray for me, that I may be worthy of your trust."

Later, as the crowd began to thin and conversations turned to holiday preparations, Father Mark noticed a young couple standing off to the side—a beautiful woman with kind eyes and a child cradled in her arms, and beside her, a man in a crisp jacket with the energy of someone about to embark on a long journey.

Father Mark's heart lifted. Young families gave him hope— living proof that faith could still be passed down.

He approached them with an open smile.

"Peace be with you. I'm Father Mark."

The woman stepped forward, graceful and confident.

"Ana," she said. "This is my husband, Miguel, and our daughter, Maria."

Father Mark knelt slightly, smiling at the little girl, who shyly buried her face in her mother's coat.

"You have a beautiful family," he said warmly.

As he stood, he caught a whisper between Ana and Miguel: "His visa finally came. He flies to the U.S. tomorrow."

The words struck a chord.

Another separation. Another marriage put on hold by oceans and opportunity.

As Father Mark rose to his full height, he felt his clerical collar shift slightly out of place. Ana, noticing, reached out without hesitation, her fingers brushing his neck as she adjusted it back into alignment. A small, instinctual act—almost too intimate in its familiarity.

"Congratulations, Father," Ana said, her voice soft but resonant. "This is a wonderful parish… and you're in very good hands."

Their eyes met. Just for a moment. Long enough for something unspoken to pass between them.

He smiled—controlled, pastoral, polite.

She smiled back—gracious, respectful… but her gaze lingered.

Miguel didn't notice. He was already looking down at his phone, responding to travel details.

"Thank you," Father Mark replied, his voice smooth. "I hope we'll see you both again before your departure."

"Oh, I'll be around," Ana said, her tone light.

"Then I look forward to it."

As they walked away, Father Mark watched them disappear into the crowd. A winter breeze swept through the open doors of the parish hall, ruffling the edge of his cassock. He took a breath.

The priesthood was never meant to be easy. His collar now sat snug against his throat again—restored to its place.

But beneath it, his pulse had quickened.

In his first homily, he had spoken about leadership, grace, and humility. About the weight of the cross and the call to serve.

Now, alone at the threshold of this new assignment, he whispered to himself:

"Lord, give me strength… not only to guide them, but to guard myself."

Outside, the snow began to fall softly again—like a benediction.

A new chapter had begun.

THE END.

EPILOGUE

A year after Ava and her children moved into their long-awaited home, grief arrived uninvited. Adam's parents passed away—quietly, unexpectedly, just months apart. Ava lit candles and wept alone in the new house they had dreamed of building together. Across the ocean, Adam received the news with a trembling hand but did not return for the funerals. Bound by the final stages of his permanent residency process in the United States, and perhaps by his own pride, he vowed never to go back.

Ava continued with her life in the only way she knew how—faithfully, gently, and alone. She still saw Father Mark now and then, and more often, Joseph. With each meeting came fleeting moments of warmth, even flirtation—soft shadows of affection that never fully took shape. Hope had quietly slipped from her heart. She no longer believed Adam would return. She stopped speaking his name aloud.

Father Mark, ever perceptive, saw her resignation and offered her something she hadn't considered: freedom. He told her Adam had abandoned her, spiritually and morally. "He is not coming back, Ava," he said one evening, his voice both soothing and persuasive. "You deserve a new life. A real one." Through connections within the diocese, he offered a pathway to annul her marriage—an official, ecclesiastical erasure of the bond that once defined her. All it would cost was ten thousand dollars. Ava blinked in disbelief. It had never occurred to her that such a thing was even possible. But possible didn't mean affordable. And so, the option remained a cruel irony—freedom, just beyond her reach.

In America, Adam's life had shifted again. With the help of the attorneys Mary worked for, he finalized his legal residency. It was those same attorneys who introduced him to a priest known for 'resolving difficult matters.' For ten thousand dollars—coincidentally, or perhaps not—his marriage to Ava was annulled. There was no call, no explanation. Just paperwork. Silence. And then, freedom.

Mary, too, had made her decision. After learning her husband back home had fathered a child with another woman, she quietly closed that chapter of her life. She would not return. With Adam by her side and the legal entanglements behind them, she began planning their second marriage—this time, in the Church.

Back in the village, Father Mark thrived. The burdens of priesthood never seemed to weigh on him the way they did on others. With a new associate to share the daily duties, he managed to juggle the roles of pastor, chaplain, confidant, and—privately—something more. Every two years, a new luxury car gleamed in his driveway. Parishioners adored him, praised his sermons, and spoke quietly of his bright future. "He'll be a bishop someday," they said with pride.

And though he was busy, Father Mark still found time. Time to write. To call. To visit. Ana's name appeared in his calendar often. And occasionally, Ava's.

Not everything ends with a confession.